XL-ENCE

XL-ENCE

The Human Development Project

Patti Mobile

Printed in the United States of America
Published in Hellertown, PA

Cover design by Patti Mobile
Library of Congress Control Number 2024921593
ISBN 979-8-89420-025-5

For more information or to place bulk orders,
contact the author or the publisher
at Jennifer@BrightCommunications.net.

To my father, Simon Galen, who inspired me to use my imagination. He believed that dreaming and working for a better future would change the world. And for all the people who believe that in their hearts, there is nothing that can stop us from making the world a better place.

Prologue

Dear Hannah,

Our beautiful planet has nearly reached the tipping point: the point where there is no turning back. I can't explain how I know this, but it is true. Something must be done to change the balance. But I need help, your help. Sixty billion dollars might seem like a lot of money. Actually, it is just enough to light the spark. I've spent many years looking for the right person to handle this challenge. You may think you're just an ordinary middle-school teacher. However, you're the only person with the qualities we need in this moment.

This isn't an easy task—to reshape the future for humanity. We must find a way. And so, I entrust this $60 billion to you. The time left to change from this path is short, and I will provide as much guidance as I can. Find the inspiration, the bravery, and the strength that I know are inside you.

Good luck,

Your benefactor and friend

Hannah quickly flopped down in her favorite green leather chair in the living room of her condo and gasped. She reached for the envelope and turned it over. *Postmarked in Denver, Colorado. No return address. I don't know anyone who lives in Denver.*

Maybe I missed something in the letter. Reading it again provided little clarity. Suddenly, Hannah's living room felt like a small square box where strange and unusual things happened. Then her cell phone rang on the table next to her chair. Even though she didn't recognize the number, she automatically reached to answer the call.

"Hello?" Hannah asked, her voice creaking like a rusty chain.

"Good afternoon. My name is Dirk Jackson. I am a senior partner in the law firm of Jackson, Montgomery, and Sheffield. Am I speaking with Hannah Larsen?" His voice was deep and resonant, but when Hannah tried to answer, nothing happened. She cleared her throat.

"Yes, I am Hannah Larsen. Why are you calling me?"

"Did you receive an unusual letter? We have been hired to administer funds upward of $60 billion dollars to you provided by an anonymous benefactor. There are certain conditions that must be met to release the funds. I suggest that you meet with us as soon as possible. I believe that you live in Columbus, Ohio. Is that right?"

"Mr. Jackson ... before I start giving you details about where I live or anything else, I need to know what is happening. Who is this mysterious benefactor? Why was I chosen? I find it easier to believe that this is some kind of elaborate practical joke."

Dirk Jackson chuckled at that. "I'm sure it seems that way. As a matter of fact, other than verifying that the funds are, indeed, completely legitimate, we have no idea who's given the money to you. As to why you were chosen, only your benefactor can answer that question. We've received specific instructions regarding how to handle the funds. We'll provide information and assistance to you as needed. There will be further communication from your benefactor later. There are documents that need to be signed, including verification of your identity, and setting up access to our staff for legal advice." He paused and waited for Hannah to speak.

This still feels like a joke or a scam. I'd better check this out before I agree to anything, Hannah thought but merely said, "Continue."

"Please consider this the start of a working relationship. I would advise you to keep your windfall confidential at present to give you some time to consider how to move forward. It is your decision whether to accept this gift. However, I understand that there are time constraints. That's why I suggested we meet soon."

"Sorry, but I'm going to do some research first. I will call you back when and *if* I am convinced you're not a scam artist."

Sure enough, Jackson, Montgomery, and Sheffield appeared right away in Hannah's Google search. The law firm had offices in New York, Chicago, and California. Dirk Jackson Sr. was the president of the firm. His son managed the Chicago and New York offices as senior partner.

So far, so good. I wish I knew who this benefactor is or was. Maybe if I knew more about him (or her), I could figure out what he (or she) wants me to do. What about teaching? The more Hannah thought about her job, the more she realized it was going nowhere fast. It was the same thing, year after year. She wasn't as inspired as when she accepted the position eight years ago. Between the time demands of her job and her family, she wasn't meeting any new and interesting people. Her last romantic relationship was a dismal failure. It was so bad she decided to abstain from men until she figured out what she wanted from them. *How can I commit to a relationship when I feel so unfulfilled?*

Another thing that bothered her was the conservation crisis implicit in the letter. Although she had felt the effects of climate change living in Ohio, she knew there was a lot more going on. Turning back to the computer, she typed in "climate change." This brought up pictures of animal species that were on the verge of extinction, rain forests being cleared for crops to sell on the global market, and ice caps melting at the poles.

I've been acting as if I'm not involved in any of that, Hannah thought. *As long as I have food on the table, I have a roof over my head, and my family is safe, I've able to push that information aside. Time to ask more questions.* Hannah called the phone number for the law firm listed on the internet.

"Hello, this is Hannah Larsen for Dirk Jackson," she said, then waited, listening to their cheesy hold music.

"I'm so glad you called, Ms. Larsen. Do you have any questions for us?" Dirk asked when he finally answered the call.

"Probably more questions than you have time to answer. But, I think we should meet. Are you available on Saturdays? Could we meet around 9 a.m. Ohio time?" she asked.

"Yes to both questions. Can you suggest a location where you will feel comfortable?"

"Let's meet in the lobby of Huntington Bank in Columbus. Text me anything you want me to bring to our meeting." She placed her thumb on the "Off" button of her cell phone and pressed hard.

Her heart was racing ... $60 billion! To bring the world back from the tipping point. *What did that mean?* Suddenly, her mind was filled with images of massive forest fires, parents and children crying in the parking lot after a school mass shooting, wars initiated by people who never stopped to listen to each other, and water and air pollution. *How can I possibly change all of that?* she wondered, pacing around her kitchen, trying to organize her thoughts. Three things were clear: She couldn't give up the chance to be in control of $60 billion, especially for this cause; she needed a great plan; and her life would never be the same. Hannah stopped pacing, realizing that she had decided to accept the challenge.

Chapter 1: Hannah's Normal Life

Three weeks after meeting with the lawyers, Hannah had read through a massive amount of paperwork and submitted all of the documents they requested to verify her identity. She felt the conviction to change the world starting to build inside her. It left her with an empty feeling that she decided to fill with a hot fudge sundae.

Then, after a busy day teaching her students about the flaws in ancient Roman politics, Hannah dragged her laptop into her condominium, dropping the mail into the basket in the kitchen. *Midweek, and I'm already worn out!* She glanced over at the red blinking light on the answering machine. The caller ID showed Maya, her older sister, had left a message.

"Bobby wants to know if Aunt Hannah can come to his soccer game this afternoon. It's at Jeffrey Anderson Park, 4:30. We'll be on the west field under the blue tarp. Bring something to drink; all the snacks are for the kids. See you there!"

Why not? I haven't seen them in a couple of weeks, Hannah thought. She went to change into some casual clothes. On the old oak dresser were the most recent pictures of her family. Maya; her husband, James; Bobby, eight; and little Chelsea, five, were smiling back at her in their Christmas finery. Grandma Marjorie and Grandpa Neil Larsen's picture was on the left side in a tarnished silver frame. Their photo had been taken at the seashore when they were all together in North Carolina about five years ago. She looked up, noticing what everyone else did; her eyes were the same grey-blue as Grandpa Neil's, and her rosy cheeks with the dimple in the left one were just like Grams's. Hannah didn't mind. They were her favorite people anyway.

Hannah scrambled into a pair of blue walking shorts, a flowered golf shirt, and sandals before grabbing her keys to run out the door. *What an incredible spring afternoon! It would be perfect for archery practice—no wind and 75 degrees, and the middle of the week. The range would be empty.* But she knew that there was no time for archery today; her niece and nephew would completely occupy her time until she was ready to return home.

Hannah loved the way Bobby included her in all his activities; his natural enthusiasm revitalized her when she felt that her students had all but drained hers. Chelsea was the quiet one, except when it came to music. She could sing any melody she heard. Grandpa Neil gave her a little, hand-carved pipe last year when she turned four. And now she was never without it. She crafted lively tunes to greet the day and lullabies to follow the sun past the horizon. For Hannah, her niece was a never-ending source of wonder.

Hannah finally found a parking space. After locking her purse in the trunk and grabbing her water bottle, she headed to the path behind the baseball diamonds. The park's soccer fields were filled with young boys and girls. Their bright uniforms created a riot of color and movement that caught the eye. Hannah found herself on the opposite side of the field from Maya when she arrived. She was on the side with the coach and other players from Bobby's team. The scoreboard showed a 3 - 3 tie. The players seemed to be very evenly matched. But then Hannah noticed a girl with shiny brown hair from Bobby's team streak forward with the ball. Bobby trailed about five feet behind her. He broke to her right, anticipating a pass as they moved the ball down the field.

The girl was having no trouble keeping the soccer ball away from the defenders. She seemed to cut around them as if they were standing still, and by the time they reacted to her movements, she was too far away to catch. Bobby ran forward, trying to keep up with her. The goalie for the opposing team was a tall, athletic boy. He watched the girl's movements intently. He blocked a good portion of the goal entrance area. Getting the ball by him would take some skill. The girl was almost there. She had a slight smile on her face, looking directly at the goalie. When she was about two feet away from him, she dropped to the ground, sliding on her left side, and kicked the ball in with her right leg.

Cheers broke out around her as Bobby's teammates celebrated the victory goal. Hannah waved to Bobby as the team approached the sideline.

He ran into her arms chanting, "We won! We won!"

It took a while for everyone to calm down. The players lined up to shake hands, then they ran off to the family tables for their well-earned snacks.

Hannah took the opportunity to have a few words with the coach. He was about forty-five, with sandy blond hair thinning at the top, warm brown eyes, and the well-rounded belly of a man who is content with life.

"Hi. My name is Hannah. I'm Bobby's aunt," she explained as she extended her hand.

"Welcome," the coach replied. "So glad you could make it to the game. My name's Derrick Flannagan."

"The end was certainly exciting. Who is the girl that scored the last goal?" Hannah asked.

"That's Karen Jeffries. I've never coached anyone like her, and I've been coaching some of the best teams in the state for the past ten years."

"There's something about her ... I can't put my finger on it. Why do you think she's so good, Derrick?"

"I know you'll think this is crazy, but it's like she's got Jedi reflexes. She knows what other people are going to do before they act. She senses where the openings are going to be. I don't know how to explain it, but she's pretty amazing. I've been working with her for about five months, and I've run out of things to teach her." Derrick paused, looking over at a beautiful golden retriever with its leash tied around a large elm tree.

"Excuse me," Coach Derrick said, "but my wife will kill me if I don't take Buttons for her walk.

She's been tied up the whole game. Would you like to come with us?"

"Maybe for a few minutes," Hannah said. *So much talent, but with more of the world being destroyed every minute, where is a future for an athletic phenom like Karen? Or a musical genius like Chelsea? Could their talents be part of the solution I'm looking for?*

Hannah, Coach Derrick, and Buttons started walking along the path toward the south edge of the park. The late spring flowers perfuming the air, bright green leaves emerging on the trees, and cool afternoon breezes made spring Hannah's favorite time of year. Buttons pranced happily along at the end of her leash, content to smell the bushes and bark at the squirrels.

"You know, with the right training, Karen could be an Olympic athlete. She's got great flexibility, stamina, and lightning-fast reflexes. She could be really good at a lot of different sports. You act like a person who's good with children," Derrick said as they walked underneath the budding trees.

"I'm a middle-school history teacher," Hannah said. "And I'm always looking for better ways to teach and inspire children. So, what would it take? For Karen to reach her full potential, I mean," Hannah asked.

Derrick was quiet for a little while as they walked along. Then he found the words. "Well, for one thing, she'd need a first-class training facility with weights and a trampoline, regular workouts, and other kids who are just as good as or better than she is to challenge her. I'm a good coach, but that would be out of my league. She'd need someone with worldwide competitive experience." Excitement crept into his voice as he explained the perfect setup to her.

"Wow," Hannah said. "I see where you're going. There's nothing like that around here, is there?"

"Naw. It would cost a large fortune to build a facility like that, and the kids would have to pay a small fortune to use it. And think of the time they would have to spend there—three to four hours of training a day, scrimmages at night, and tournaments on the weekends! Then there are travel expenses, probably tutors for schoolwork, a special diet, and medical supervision for optimum growth. Even colleges don't have that kind of training program," he explained.

Hannah tried to feel out his vision, but it was solely focused on sports. She needed time to think about a bigger picture. *I have been given a large fortune, which makes a lot of things that were impossible before within reach now.*

What crazy person left me sixty billion dollars? Someone I knew in college? A teacher I used to work with? I should comb through my photo albums.

"Well, I need to join my family for dinner, Coach," Hannah said. "I appreciate everything that you've shared with me and your point of view."

"I just wish it were possible," Coach Derrick murmured. "Don't let her size fool you, Hannah. With the right opportunity, Karen Jeffries could make a huge difference in this world. Anyway, it was good talking with you, too." He pulled Buttons to his side and headed toward the parking lot.

Chapter 2: A $60 Billion Idea

The idea kept getting bigger the more Hannah thought about it. She needed a sounding board, someone she knew and trusted, someone who could look past his or her own private life to see the possibilities.

How much should I reveal about the amount of money involved? That could get me in a lot of trouble. Should I talk to Maya?

The sisters were almost too close. Hannah had been ten when the car crash that killed their father nearly crippled Maya for life. When the accident happened, Hannah had been at home, watching over their sick mother.

A neighbor had driven Hannah to the hospital. Although she had never been to a hospital before, Hannah was drawn to the intensive care unit like a magnet.

Maya was unconscious, covered with bloody bandages, her legs dangling from straps attached to a metal runner in the ceiling. She was told that Maya had minute fractures along her spine that *might* heal if she was very lucky.

Maya's life is not going to be snuffed out at thirteen years old, Hannah thought.

It didn't matter what the doctors said from then on. Hannah was determined that Maya was going to get well. They spent the next three years working together through physical therapy, two corrective surgeries, and bouts of depression. But Maya healed, growing stronger every week, and Hannah always had a smile for her. Much later, Maya told Hannah that if it hadn't been for her constant encouragement, she would have given up the fight.

No, Hannah thought. *Maya wouldn't be objective, no matter what crazy idea I come up with. And the money ... so much money. She probably wouldn't even believe it.*

Now Hannah's thoughts turned to Grams and Grandpa Larsen. They were always into some new project or other. Increasing their experiences, learning new things, and keeping an open mind was their philosophy of life. They were good at figuring things out.

Grams was the astronomer, the herbalist, the healer, and the chef. Just thinking about dinners at their cabin in Maine made Hannah's mouth water.

Grandpa Neil had worked with his hands from the time he was a little boy—so her father had told her. He built the most amazing furniture, gadgets, and even stained glass lamps. Grandpa Neil exuded peacefulness. He was quiet and thoughtful, but nothing escaped his gentle scrutiny. He was Hannah's teacher when she couldn't unravel an explanation from her textbooks.

Considering their wide range of talents, Grams and Grandpa Neil were probably the perfect sounding board for Hannah. She decided to call them to see when they were available. She started pacing around the kitchen, waiting for them to answer. *Come on, Grams. Please, be there.*

"Happy Wednesday. How is the teaching business?" Hannah could picture her grandmother's face smiling on the other end of the line. "So nice of you to give us a call during the week."

"Hey, Grams. How are you and Grandpa Neil?"

"Couldn't be better. We've been mucking around in the garden, getting it ready for planting. What's new?"

"I have a lot to tell you, but not over the phone. Something BIG has happened to me, nothing bad," Hannah was quick to squelch that thought. "Do you think I could come out and stay with you for a couple of days? I'd like to talk with you and Grandpa Neil. I need perspective and clear thinking."

"Well, isn't that mysterious? You have certainly piqued my interest. I'd better check with Neil. But we can always make time for you. Why not make your travel plans and call back later to confirm?"

"You're the best, Grams. Thanks so much. I'll call back by 9:00 this evening. Love you," Hannah said, then put the phone down and collapsed into her favorite green leather chair. *This is the answer. It just feels right.* She called the school and arranged to take a few days off work. She would arrive in Maine on Saturday morning if she caught the red-eye from Columbus.

✦ ✦ ✦

Hannah drove the car she rented in Bangor north along State Highway 2. When she reached the turnoff, she slowed down along the winding road to her grandparents' home. Dappled sunshine reached through the leaves and felt warm on her face; the morning breeze was fresh with the smell of growing things. She loved the feeling of driving away from the busyness of the city, leaving her frustration, tension, and doubts behind.

During the phone call with Grams, she remembered hearing Grandpa Neil say, "Now, Marjorie, you just let Hannah get here when she gets here. She knows the way."

Thank goodness he understands, thought Hannah. *I need transition time.*

Hannah kept rehearsing how to explain her idea. The more she thought about it, the more detailed it became. She shook her head, letting her chestnut brown hair fly back in the wind. *Relax, Hannah. No one is going to judge you here.*

It took only an hour to reach the Larsens' beautiful chalet tucked in among the pine trees. Grandpa was leaning against a hoe, surveying the neat rows gently carved into the soft earth of the garden. He was in a green-and-red flannel shirt with the sleeves rolled up, jeans, and hiking boots. His wavy gray hair had been cut short on the sides. He wiped the sweat from his brow with his forearm, and then he turned to welcome Hannah as she stepped from the car.

"What's cooking in that head of yours?" he asked as he reached for her suitcase.

"Too much, Grandpa Neil," Hannah said. "Look at the garden! It's twice as big as the one you had last year. You plan on feeding most of Kennebec County this summer?" she teased.

"We might," he teased back. "Let's go see what your grandma made for lunch. I'm starving."

"Me, too," Hannah said as they headed toward the kitchen.

Lunch was homemade vegetable soup, cheese sandwiches with apple slices on fresh whole grain bread, and lemonade. They ate in companionable silence at the red oak kitchen table Grandpa had made as a present for Grams long ago on their fifth anniversary. After cleaning up, they all went to the front porch to relax and drink more lemonade. Grams sat with Grandpa Neil in the swinging rocker seat, waiting for Hannah to speak.

Hannah finished her lemonade, setting the empty glass down on the small table next to the Adirondack chair she always sat in. She closed her eyes, clearing away the random thoughts that usually distracted her.

After a moment, Hannah began her story. "I've been thinking about the evolution of human beings—about the skills, traits, and knowledge we must develop to solve today's disasters and continue our existence far into the future."

She watched as her grandparents' eyes grew round with surprise. They probably weren't expecting a philosophical speech about the growth of humankind.

"Follow me for a few minutes," Hannah said. "Darwin's research showed that natural selection encourages genetic traits that predispose a species to survive. But evolution is very, very slow, occurring over many generations. Given the scope of challenges we face, we don't have that kind of time. But there might be ways to speed up that evolution. The strange thing is, I think that it's already starting to happen." Hannah watched their faces. Grams's eyes were sparkling, and the little dimple in her cheek appeared for a brief second.

"Go on," Grandpa Neil encouraged her.

Hannah sighed. "Some of our survival traits are really nasty—violence, greed, self-involvement. But if we could develop other positive traits, such as empathy and understanding, that would give us a clear advantage without having to destroy other people in the process ...," Hannah paused, groping for the right words. "This is where it starts getting complicated. I'm trying to think of a way to encourage the development of positive human traits, without genetic manipulation, by naturally stimulating each individual's potential for excellence. To accelerate the process, my idea is to find people who already have special traits—like enhanced perception—then to challenge them and help them to strengthen those traits quickly. I believe that children are the key."

Hannah wasn't sure where to go from this point. Grams was nodding her head, shaking the gray hair loose from her headband. She had more laugh lines around her mouth and eyes, but her eyes still twinkled like stars. Grandpa Neil leaned forward, putting his elbows on his knees, and resting his chin in his hands.

"So, how do you think that can be done?" he asked.

"At first, I thought of a huge training camp. I got the idea from Bobby's soccer coach, Derrick

Flannagan. But that would limit the scope to only physical skill development. What about someone like Chelsea? She has some pretty extraordinary talents; she practically hears music in the rustle of her notebook paper. And what about people like my friend Olivia? She not only manages the Economic Development Department at Ohio State, but is also a mathematical genius. The way she sees how things relate to each other is ... well, it's amazing. There needs to be a place ... a place where Challenges can be set up to bring out the human potential for greatness. And here's the weird part. Hold on to your hats." Hannah paused to put the words together in a way that would make sense.

"I received a letter and was contacted by a law firm regarding a gift of sixty billion dollars to use for a very special purpose. The letter stressed that we are destroying the world, and we must start changing that right now." Hannah took a deep breath and waited for them to comment.

Grandpa Neil was the first to speak after a long period of silence. "That must have been quite a shock, Hannah. Who would give you such a large fortune? And why select you to save the world?"

"I wish I knew, Grandpa Neil. Maybe I'll figure it out later. I have documentation from a law firm called Jackson, Montgomery, and Sheffield, proving that the funds are real and have been set aside for the purpose of reversing the damage people are causing to the world. Even you and I know that the flooding is getting worse here. Remember the grass fires two years ago in Canada? I can't pass up this opportunity to try to help," Hannah insisted.

"I see that you've been thinking about what can be done. Where most people would be reaching for technology, you've chosen a different path. Why is that?" Grandpa Neil asked.

"Technology is too easy," Hannah said. "Plus, it places a barrier between us and the natural world, the world we are destroying. We have to slow down the way we think about doing things and use the resources within us. We're not connected to the land, the plants and animals, or each other the way we need to be to stop creating more damage. Is this making any sense to you?" she asked anxiously.

"Lordy, child! Don't start doubting yourself now," Grams said emphatically. "There will always be people who'll tell you 'it can't be done.' But where would we be if Marie Curie, Harriet Tubman, or Albert Einstein had given up on their dreams before they even started?"

Grandpa Neil just sat there with a big grin on his face. "You don't dream small, do you, Hannah?"

"It makes sense," Grams said. "It's really quite astonishing to look at things the way you've just presented them. And I'm not sure where you're headed with all this. But that's why you're here, isn't it? To test your ideas out on us."

Hannah felt herself flush. How well they knew her! She took a deep breath and looked into their eyes, her gaze steadier than she felt inside. "Yes, I'm going to use you both shamelessly. This quest demands a certain amount of, well not ruthlessness, but supreme dedication. The next couple of days are going to be hell-on-earth for me, but I intend to hammer this dream into reality."

$$\star \; \star \; \star$$

The next day when Hannah came downstairs for some coffee, she found Grams sitting at the kitchen table. "Want some coffee or tea, Grams?" Hannah asked as she opened the cabinet for the mugs.

"No, thanks. Too much coffee makes me jumpy," Grams said.

"So, what's going on with you and Grandpa Neil?"

Grams leaned forward and laced her fingers together on the table. Hannah pulled her chair closer so that she could watch her face as they talked.

"We're getting older, you know. I'm trying to get Neil to slow down some. I was hoping that we could travel, but there are always projects around the house and land that keep us here. When you started talking about how the world is being destroyed, I realized how isolated we've become. We are connected to the land and our community here, but we don't tune in to what's happening in the rest of the world."

"I was blissfully unaware of the massive damage myself until recently," Hannah said. "This little part of the world ... it's been your life since you both retired. I get that things are changing, and adjusting is hard sometimes. How about this, Grams? I can pay you and Grandpa Neil as advisors on this project of mine, and then you can use the money to hire a handyman."

"Money's not the problem," Grams said. "But I do like the idea of hiring a handyman or woman. I think we just need to talk it out between us. Neil can think of it as mentoring. He has always loved teaching. Well, you know all about that, don't you?" Grams smiled and patted Hannah's cheek. "Sounds like you would be willing to leave your teaching job for this. Is that what you want?"

"You know I love teaching, too. But schools are no longer about inspiring children to learn and share ideas. Education is becoming more about money and pushing the children out into the world than making them better citizens of it. I can't support that system any longer. This challenge woke me up."

"I'm glad you told me how you feel. But we better get breakfast on the table. I can hear your stomach rumbling, and I'm hungry, too."

Flapjacks, blackberry jam, and scrambled eggs found their way to the table in short order. While they talked over breakfast, Hannah started making lists in her head for the next steps of the project. She knew that her grandparents would ask the right questions to keep her on track to develop her ideas. So, later that day, they started talking about the tough parts. Because Hannah knew she would need help managing the $60 billion, financial advisors were at the top of the list. Grandpa Neil kept shaking his head and drawing his brown and grey bushy eyebrows together.

"Listen, Hannah. That much money is going to attract some awful people to you—greedy businessmen, politicians, religious fanatics, and scam artists of all kinds. You need some sharp cookies on your team, like your friend Olivia. She won't let anyone pull the wool over your eyes."

Hannah felt like she had been punched in the gut. *He's right. What do I know about dealing with scam artists? Nothing! I need protection, but how?*

Grams stood up and grabbed Hannah's hands. "I know you are going to face things you've never had to think about before. Just remember that you're not alone. To start with, you can tell people you are working on a child development project. You won't attract the wrong kinds of people with that description. Working with children just doesn't pay. If you save the salary information until later, based on qualifications, you'll get all kinds of applicants. Then you can select the people who seem to fit best with the project goals."

Hannah squeezed Grams's hands, standing up to give her a big hug. "You're right. I'm going to ask the lawyers for recommendations for financial management consultants. They can help vet the most qualified applicants. I need to use the resources I have to make good decisions so this project can start out right."

Chapter 3: The Key Players

A few weeks after the conference with her grandparents, Hannah called lawyer Dirk Jackson, asking him to meet her in a conference room she had reserved at Ohio State University through her friend, Olivia Hutchins. The conference room was nothing special, a round table with six wheeled chairs around it.

Before Hannah began speaking, she thought, *I wish I could describe how this project will slow the damage we are creating in the world, but I just can't see it yet. It's only a possibility right now.*

"I realize that you probably were expecting more specific details," Hannah said. "But the fact is, the project will become more solid as we move forward. It's the people who become involved who will define it. If we're going to create a better future, we need to start by creating better people."

Dirk was oddly quiet, but Hannah saw a twinkle in his dark eyes.

"What are you thinking right now, Mr. Jackson?" Hannah felt her heart racing. *Don't panic now, Hannah! Just breathe. Wait for him to answer.*

"I do wish that you had a concrete plan, but that's what lawyers are all about. I'm limited in the assistance I can provide, but I suggest that you need a Finance Team, and the sooner the better. We can make one million dollars available for recruiting personnel during the first six months.

I can also provide you with standard contract agreements that will protect you in the world of international finance," Dirk explained. "How does that sound to you?"

"Exactly where I thought I should start as well. Do you have any recommendations? Or maybe the bank could suggest a few candidates. If you could provide a list of qualifications, I'll develop the questions for us to discuss. I have to imagine it takes years to develop trust before you let someone handle billions of dollars. And I don't have any time to waste." *He should be able to give me what I need to start with this,* Hannah thought.

"We can certainly give you some referrals," Dirk said. "And the bank can as well. You need more than a financial advisor, though. You need someone who will take time to teach you, support you, and be honest with you. I'll send you a short list and some questions to help you get started. But, once again, start as soon as you can. The clock is ticking."

After weeks of phone calls, Hannah realized the strongest candidate was Stephen Goldfarb, president of the Union Royal Bank in London. She told him about her need for a financial team to help secure her wealth, build for the future, and provide advice for opportunities to make her project into a reality. During their interview, Hannah saw that he was excited about helping her to manage such a large fortune. He explained that there was an enormous amount of information to learn. Hannah recorded their conversations and took some online classes in financial management and investing.

Hannah talked with Stephen about the kinds of people she needed on her team. Stephen arranged for interviews at various branches of his bank, including travel to Switzerland, China, Brazil, and other countries, so that she could speak to people with global experience and talent in the world of finance.

After four weeks of researching and interviewing, Hannah was ready to make some decisions. Although it was after 11:00 p.m., she couldn't wait to call Stephen.

"Hello, Stephen. Did I wake you?" she asked.

He grumbled something that sounded like, "Mmmmff. Grrrrrhhd."

Hannah started laughing.

"So, you think this is funny?" sputtered Stephen. "It's bloody four in the morning here. Where are you?"

"Oh dear! I'm in Ohio. I forgot about the time difference. Are you awake enough to listen for a few minutes?"

"I guess so, but you might have to tell me again later."

"At first, after looking at banks and investment companies, I kept thinking that I needed a lot of people on the Finance Team. But then I realized that they are managing money for a lot of people. This Finance Team is only for me and my project. So, we don't really need a lot of people, do we?"

"Hmmm. That is essentially correct. We would need about five people. Three or four would not be enough to cross-check and prevent bad decisions. Six or seven would be overkill. Do you have any candidates in mind?" Stephen asked, fully awake now.

"I would like to recruit my best friend, Olivia Hutchins," Hannah said. "She is a mathematical genius and works at Ohio State University. I see her in the role of Chief Operations Officer, but she'll take some convincing. The other candidate I liked was Nicholai Resenden. I talked with him at his bank in Turkey. And how do you feel about one of the lawyers from Jackson, Montgomery, and Sheffield?"

"I don't think the law firm can take a position in the project. It would be a conflict of interest for them," Stephen told her. "Let me look over your notes from the interviews. Oh, what did you think of Lei Chen Xiao?"

"At first, I thought he was scatterbrained based on the state of his clothing. He looked like he slept on the train coming into the city, although he certainly has impressive credentials, teaching financial management at Tianjin University. He spoke so concisely, and yet, he made me feel completely at ease. I don't think the best place for him is on the financial team. But there is definitely a place for him in the project. I see him working with people, not with investments." Hannah was anxious to wrap the decisions up. It was time to initiate the next phase of the project.

"Okay, Hannah. You work on Olivia. I'll talk to Nicholai. Damn you! I guess starting a few hours early won't kill me. The sacrifices I make for you!" Stephen grumbled, and then he hung up.

Hannah chuckled. She appreciated his sense of humor. If she was looking for an older brother or a fussy uncle, Stephen would fit the role perfectly. Hannah was glad that Stephen didn't hold back when talking to her about her choices. She had no idea what that much money could do, but she was determined to find out.

Chapter 4: Olivia Hutchins

Hannah hoped she could convince Olivia to become part of the project. Olivia was extremely intelligent, with degrees in both chemistry and physics.

She remembered when they first met at the archery range at Ohio State University. Hannah was a much better archer than Olivia, and Olivia stopped her practice that day to study Hannah's technique. Hannah blushed bright red when she realized she was being watched. Olivia laughed and apologized for being so rude.

For Olivia, everything boiled down to formulas, rules, and calculations. Hannah tried to see her point of view, but there was more to being good at something. There was a connection to the archer, how the person felt as they pulled back the bow, and when they knew the right moment to let the arrow fly. With Olivia's skills in observation and analysis, she would be able to oversee a complex project. Hannah was also hoping that her university connections would support the recruitment of academic professionals, research assistants, technology developers, and pioneers in many fields.

After many phone calls, Olivia finally agreed to meet with Hannah to discuss her project, *if* she committed to spending at least sixty minutes at the archery range first. Hannah eagerly agreed.

Getting out into the sunshine and fresh air for a while was just what she needed to relax. And improving her skills would put Olivia in a good mood afterward.

That morning, the range was almost empty. While the friends set up and prepared their targets, a stiff wind blew in from the north. *Nothing is more challenging than shooting arrows in a gusting wind,* Hannah thought. Olivia quickly tied her long brown hair back, and Hannah did the same. *No stray hairs to distract from the target.*

"Are you ready?" Olivia challenged.

"Let's go!" Hannah cried.

After they finished, they tallied the point count, and Hannah had barely edged out Olivia. "Wow! You've really improved," Hannah told her.

"I've worked hard, trying to incorporate some of your techniques. But this wind made it really exciting."

"I could sure go for a basket of onion rings right now," Hannah replied. "Holding the bow steady in the wind always makes me hungry."

"Pack up. Lunch awaits!" Olivia noted, unstringing her bow.

They went to lunch at the most popular restaurant near Ohio State, placing an order for iced tea, onion rings, and turkey club sandwiches. Sitting outside under a giant elm tree, Hannah told Olivia about the letter from her benefactor, detailing the challenge to bring the world back from the tipping point that could destroy everything. Hannah said that at first, she didn't see what could be done and felt like it was an impossible task—even with the money she was being given. She went on to explain that later, with help from her grandparents, she thought that a way could be found: If people, especially children, could develop stronger, more positive traits like empathy and a deeper connection to the environment, maybe that would create a different future for humankind.

As Hannah spoke, Olivia waggled her eyebrows to signal she was paying attention and catching on. Both of the friends ate while Hannah talked.

"I know that doesn't explain the situation very well," Hannah said. "When I thought it out, I realized that industrialization was what started separating people from each other and from the Earth. Native peoples all over the world are deeply connected to their environments, living in harmony. The skills they used so often began to fade away when machines started to do the work and technology took over providing information." Hannah stopped talking and ate her sandwich, watching Olivia's face for clues to how she felt.

After one of the busboys cleared the table, Olivia wiped her mouth and sighed.

"Hannah, this sounds like a fever dream! Who would give you enough money to do that? There are only a few people in the world who have that kind of money. This idea of yours doesn't make much sense." Olivia paused, running her hands through her shaggy, light brown hair. "I don't think I've told you much about my childhood, have I?"

Hannah shook her head, so Olivia continued. "I grew up in a very unstable household. My parents were hippies—no rules, no structure, they believed everything would work out fine. In school, I was constantly teased by other children because I wore weird clothing and shoes and brought eggplant sandwiches for lunch—yuck! When I was a teenager, I had a mouth full of crooked teeth and a face full of pimples. No one wanted to be my friend." Olivia choked up, then cleared her throat. "So, I had to learn to take care of myself. I had to earn money for braces and a dermatologist for my acne. I took odd jobs after school, saved birthday and Christmas money from my grandparents, and took over handling the family finances. I stopped listening to my parents, who were almost always high on pot and often running around the house naked." Olivia paused, using her napkin to wipe her nose. "I learned to question first and do my research before taking action."

A few tears trickled down Hannah's cheeks. She reached for Olivia's hand and held it between her own. "How awful. No wonder you are so good at everything you do. You had to be to survive. I'm sorry that I never asked you about your childhood. There are still many questions about the project that need to be answered. But I don't think I can do this without your help."

Olivia shook her head. "What you are talking about is huge! Do you realize how crazy this sounds? First, how are you going to find these remarkable people, these exceptional children? Then how will you develop those positive traits in them? And even if you can do all of that, how can you do it quickly enough to make a difference? I can't even imagine how much money all of that would take."

"Sixty billion dollars to start," Hannah told her. Olivia just stared at her. Hannah's heart dropped as she considered that she might be losing her best friend's support. "Olivia, what's going through your head? Please tell me."

"Who is crazy enough to give you sixty billion dollars?" Olivia's eyes grew big and round. "I'm not exactly tied down to my job or to this place. I'm flattered that you'd like me to be a part of this, but I've never handled anything as big as what you are proposing to do. And I have serious concerns. With so much money at stake, what if I screw up? I need a lot more information before I decide to turn my life upside down and take on a project as immense and risky as this."

If we screw up, the money will be taken away, and the world will be that much closer to oblivion. And it will be my fault that I couldn't make anyone believe it could be done, Hannah thought. Olivia was right. Hannah did not have answers. She didn't know what was required to bring the world back from the tipping point. She was trusting her gut, knowing that having intelligent, competent, and determined people like Olivia involved would be necessary for the project to succeed.

"I wish I could see a better way forward, Olivia. Your childhood showed that doing nothing won't make things better. We must act! The people who join us in this project will want to believe they can make a difference. They are the key to making a better future for us. There will be successes and failures, and we will learn more from each of them. We'll be moving one step at a time. Like most successful systems, there will have to be checks and balances that will prevent us from making bad choices. I only ask that you take some time to think about it. You've always been honest with me. I trust you and value your insights."

Olivia took a deep breath and said, "Hannah, you're just about the best friend I have. I probably need to know more about you, too. As the Eternal Skeptic, I'll email you some questions that need to be answered before I can make my decision."

With that, Olivia left $25.00 on the table, picked up her purse, winked at Hannah, and walked away.

Hannah realized she was trembling. *Shake it off, Hannah. There's work to do.*

Chapter 5: The Project Structure

The next day, Olivia sent Hannah ten questions about the project she had designed to turn the planet back from the tipping point. Hannah felt that she could reasonably answer questions about where, when, and why, but the question of how made her do some deep thinking. Instead of trying to figure out the details, she invited Olivia to spend the weekend at her condo so that they could work on it together.

Hannah knew the best approach to take with Olivia was similar to the one she used to construct lesson plans for her students. Hannah wanted to light them up inside, making them eager to learn something new. And Hannah knew that she needed a much clearer picture about the structure of the project for it to succeed.

When Olivia arrived at Hannah's, the condo living room was filled with easels, writing pads, whiteboards, colored markers, pens, and tape.

"Did you drag your entire classroom over for us?" Olivia asked.

"We might need all this stuff to figure out what will work and what won't. I've designated whiteboards for *Positively Yes, Good but Need More Info,* and *Might Work.* I would like to start with your suggestions. We'll both decide which category it goes in. Then it's my turn to bring up suggestions. How does that sound to you?"

"I'm willing to give it a try. But we only have two days, Hannah. If there are too many suggestions on the *Might Work* board and not enough on the others, I'll seriously consider going home. There are lots of successful business models you can use. Why not consider those first?" Olivia argued.

Hannah said, "Let me think about that for a minute. Would you like some coffee, tea, or juice?"

"Coffee for me—the working woman's fuel," she replied.

Hannah went into the kitchen and arranged a tray with coffee, milk, and sugar, and bottles of water for both of them. She returned to the living room, set down the tray on the maple coffee table, then reached for a bright blue marker, tapping it against her palm.

"There are parts of successful business models that can be incorporated. But, Olivia, think of where those models lead us, what their goals are. They are perpetuating a system that's making money more important than people or the planet. We must get away from that. The success of this project will be measured differently." Hannah handed Olivia a marker. "Let's write out some of your ideas. Milk in your coffee, right?" she asked.

Olivia nodded and started walking around in front of the easels. "I think better when I walk around. I hope you're okay with that. Did your benefactor define 'the tipping point' for you?"

Hannah shook her head, raising her eyebrows to indicate that she understood where Olivia was going.

"Then I think we need to define that concept for ourselves first," Olivia said. "There are tremendous forces at work, moving the world in different directions. To make changes, the project has to exert an equally strong force. Let's talk about what the tipping point is."

Hannah had done her research after she received the letter, and had learned that economic development was the driving factor, impacting education, the environment, family relationships, and individuals' physical and mental well-being. The complexity was staggering. "There were hundreds of examples when I looked up the term. But, basically, it means that ...," Hannah consulted her notes. "'There is a critical level of an external condition that induces runaway change in a system and propels it into a new state.' The applications are both positive and negative in terms of change. Scientists are trying to develop a mathematical formula that can be used to predict when the tipping point for a system will be reached." Hannah stopped, trying to see if she could add anything else, when Olivia jumped in.

"In other words, there's a critical point in a process or system beyond which a significant and maybe irreversible change takes place. Let's look at what the external conditions are now," Olivia suggested.

Hannah took a deep breath. "In most of the examples, economic development exerted the most pressure on a system. When the purpose of the development was driven by monetary gain, little attention was paid to the impact of the development on other systems, like the environment. Controls were only put in place when the damage was too great to ignore. And often, what took twenty-five to thirty years to accomplish in industrial societies, took fifty to 100 years to remediate."

"Okay," Olivia commented. "I think that you have a good working definition. So, your project must counteract unregulated economic development. What you described for me over lunch the other day doesn't sound like it's going to do that. How are a bunch of uniquely talented children going to change the drive for economic development?"

Hannah knew that Olivia would not be satisfied with a generic answer to her question. *What were some of the other examples I read about where external forces created positive change? Think, Hannah!* Hannah watched Olivia cross her arms in front of her chest and start tapping her foot. *She's right to be skeptical.*

"Olivia, it's not the drive for development that needs to be changed, it's the *method*. When people are open to learning, they'll see different ways to go forward. They can still reach their goals; maybe not as fast, but new methods will be better for their land, their health, and their future. That's the impact that we want to make. I just hope that we can get it done in time to change the balance." Hannah tried to sound more confident than she felt. She still wondered if this was the right path. But it couldn't be a coincidence that she was suddenly noticing amazing children right under her nose, such as Chelsea and soccer star Karen.

Olivia uncrossed her arms. She drank from her coffee cup as she paced around the living room, often looking up at Hannah's hopeful face. "Let's take the timing issue out of the picture for the moment. Until you define how the project will operate, we can't construct a project schedule. That's why you asked me to come over, and that's where we should go now."

Hannah was relieved to start working on the structure, rather than on conceptual topics. "How about more coffee?" she asked.

"No, thanks. I'm switching to water now. Too much coffee makes my brain go in circles," Olivia replied.

The friends brainstormed late into the evening. After calling it a night, Hannah settled Olivia into her guest bedroom, then went to bed herself.

Hannah's dreams were filled with whiteboards where she kept trying to figure out the various levels of her project and how they would interact with each other. But each dream ended with her erasing everything that was on the board and starting over.

Hannah had not been raised in a business-oriented family. She was familiar with the country's educational system, which she felt was failing badly. *Why did they never measure how successful they were in creating an enthusiasm for learning? Too afraid to see the results, obviously.* Hannah's project was going to include education and physical development, but there were no shining examples of systems for her to use as guidelines in her work

The next morning, after a quick breakfast, Hannah and Olivia resumed strategizing. Olivia took several gulps of her water and uncapped her blue marker. "I think ... finances first. Sixty billion dollars is a lot of money to manage."

"Right. Put that on the *Positively Yes* board. I have that under control because I recently interviewed a man named Stephen Goldfarb. He not only has experience handling big money for special clients, but he also has banking and international government connections. But the best part is that he's willing to take the time to train me. I have a lot to learn."

Olivia put Stephen's name next to Finance Team on the board. "How many people do you need for the team?"

"I think five people would be enough," Hannah said. "There would be me, the COO, Stephen—the CFO, and two others I am considering: Nicholai Resenden and Lei Chen Xiao."

"Well, you can add more if you need them. At least there will be several sets of eyes to monitor expenditures and help with investments," Olivia noted. "Management is next. You are the CEO, Hannah. Who else do you need, and how will you find them?"

"Start a Management Team list on the *Positively Yes* board," Hannah said. "I really want you to be the COO. It's a big responsibility, but I promise that you'll have qualified help. We'll need to recruit applicants, so determining the qualifications is critical here." Hannah put her coffee down and selected a green marker. Under the Management Team header, she started a list of traits: experience with large projects, attention to details, good communication skills, good writing skills, and working with groups.

"Let's add budget monitoring and contract processing. The Finance Team will need backup in both of those areas," Olivia said as she wrote them on the board under Hannah's list. "Do you have any Management Team candidates, other than me, in mind, Hannah?"

"I'd like to ask my sister, Maya, and her husband, James, to join the project on the Management Team. They're both excellent communicators. James is from a military family, where he learned to be flexible, organized, and disciplined. And you know Maya. Who would be a better public relations person? Maybe you could provide some recommendations?"

"That's an idea. I know several people at Ohio State who would be interested in a project like this. Of course, you need to pay them well. The benefits offered by the university system are substantial."

"Stephen has been waiting for the project structure so that he can construct a salary schedule. Then we can estimate the start-up and annual costs for personnel." Hannah picked up her water. Her thoughts kept moving away from the upper levels of the project to what she considered to be the main focus.

"We need to remember that this project is about children," Hannah said. "Too many children with unusual skills or perception meet resistance when they confide in adults. That can't happen here. There needs to be a bridge between the children and the managing adults. So, I want to explain the concept of 'Accelerators' to you now. Then we can decide which board to place it on."

"I think I want to sit down for this," Olivia said as she grabbed her water, went to the butter yellow leather couch, and sat down.

Chapter 6: Persuasive Arguments

It was Hannah's turn to pace around the living room as she gathered her thoughts to convince Olivia that this level of the project was critical. "The Accelerator group will be made up of young adults with special skills of their own," Hannah began. "They are people who can look at situations from different perspectives, who can think 'outside the box.' And they must want to mentor children. They will be the ones who will create Challenges for the children specifically designed to strengthen their unusual talents. They will also create difficult Challenges that require the children to work together to solve them.

"It will take a lot of creative thinking on our part to attract these young people," Hannah continued. "I see them as the world changers. They will take the risks and be the ones to guide the children in their new relationships. The Accelerators will be able to interface with the Management and Finance teams for direction."

"Well, this is certainly a new direction in business," Olivia said. "Based on your project concept, this would be on the *Positively Yes* board. But I think it should be on the *Good but Need More Info* board. Here's why: *Someone* needs to provide structure for the Accelerator group, to hold them accountable for getting the work done, someone to evaluate whether the Challenges they create are doing what the children need to grow. How many of these young people with special skills do you think are out there? Then, how many does the project need?" Olivia asked.

Ah, Olivia. Always so practical, and now I know why. It's also why I need her so badly. Hannah thought about her questions and opened her second bottle of water. She took a long swallow, then turned to her friend.

"I don't think I can answer those questions now. I just don't know who these people are, but I believe we can find them."

Olivia shook her head. Her shaggy brown hair fell against her cheeks, then she tucked the locks behind her ears. "Let's break for lunch. I need to think about what's been said and where to go next."

"Good idea. I have chicken and pasta salad in the fridge. We can eat on the back patio and relax for a while. Whew! I can feel the tension in my shoulders," she said, rotating her shoulders and stretching her neck muscles as they walked into the kitchen.

"I'll dish the food out for us. You can set up the patio," Olivia offered.

As they ate, conversation slowed to a bare trickle. The summer heat was almost at an end, which was just enough warmth to bake away the worries constantly plaguing Hannah to *Hurry! Hurry! Hurry!* She needed to have a clear picture in order to keep the lawyers satisfied that the project was moving forward.

Cleaning up after lunch did not take long. A pitcher of iced tea and plastic glasses replaced the coffee cups and now empty water bottles on the tray on the coffee table.

Olivia restarted the conversation. "Thanks for lunch. I love pasta salad. Now I have some more questions before we get to the lists. First, tell me about the project site. Are the children and everyone else going to live there? What is your vision for that?"

Hannah closed her eyes. As she started to explain, her voice took on a soft, dreamy quality. "I see land where there are lots of trees, mountains and small hills, meadows, streams, and native plants and animals. The site would be built on meadow flatland. There are buildings for classrooms, laboratories, medical facilities, a commissary, and dormitories. The administration building's in a separate area on the property, one more easily accessed by roads. It has conference rooms, offices, and storage areas. I see children playing soccer, swimming and boating around lakes, climbing and camping, and enjoying a barbecue pit with picnic tables. The area's away from city life. It doesn't have to be isolated from local communities, but it has a lot of land." She opened her eyes and looked at Olivia. "I think that it will cost about $250 million."

Olivia blinked a few times, then she stood and started pacing. "I see. Other people need to come there to take care of the site. Or you need to build a landing strip and hangars for planes and helicopters to transport people in and out! I don't see the project going in that direction. You are describing creating a community of people there. The goals are unique, different from the way other communities are built. The commonality is not religion, history, ethnicity, politics, or resource based. Have you thought about that?"

Hannah stood and walked to the *Good but Need More Info* board. She uncapped her green marker and wrote *Project Site* and underneath it, *Community.* "Finding a place where this project can be successful is a critical step. The first task for the Finance and Management Teams will be to locate enough land and suitable conditions for construction of the project site.

"A major challenge will be that as the weather around the world gets worse, the site we choose must be a place that is geographically sheltered," Hannah continued. "Some isolation is inevitable, just because of how much land is needed. We can control access through roads into and out of the area. However, we want to interact with local towns. Communication about the project and its goals is also a critical task. We must have support, and especially understanding, from our neighbors. The children are the key. They are the logical choice as ambassadors."

Olivia took some deep breaths. "At least you have thought about this realistically! I'm proud of you, even though you are basically a dreamer." She smiled at Hannah. The warmth of Olivia's smile always made Hannah feel special.

Hannah walked over to the *Good but Need More Info* board and wrote *Support Staff.* Olivia nodded. "Yes, cooks, janitorial staff, groundskeepers, and maintenance workers. The project must continue education in traditional areas, but maybe with different techniques? Recruitment in those fields shouldn't be as difficult as finding the Accelerators will be."

"I agree," Hannah said. "We'll be doing a lot of these tasks simultaneously. I intend to get Maya and James involved soon because of Chelsea, my niece. She is one of those extraordinary children. The Finance and Management Teams will oversee these tasks as they are progressing."

"Hmmm … screening applications is taking on a much more important role. How will you deal with non-English-speaking staff? They have to communicate with each other, the children, and everyone else at the site," Olivia pointed out.

There are just so many complications! I can't think of everything. I'm not a genius. Slow down, Hannah. That's why choosing the right people to help is where you should be now. Languages can be taught, and we will have teachers, Hannah thought before speaking. "That's a good point. We will need to hire language teachers. And language instruction software can reinforce and speed up the learning curve. So, we'll build in the process and select the languages as we need them. A lot will depend on where the project site is built." Hannah felt that working with Olivia was already making a big difference in getting the project structure developed to be successful.

Olivia nodded, then recommended, "Good. Let's get to the children next. I want to know what talents you will be looking for."

"Please write 'Children' on the *Positively Yes* board," Hannah directed. "This is another area where I don't have the vocabulary to describe what could be out there. Children with a deep connection to the environment, plants, animals, and weather patterns rise to the top of my list. Skills include empathy, precognition, observation, sensitivity, outreach, and helping skills. Look at how important this was to all native communities around the world. They recognized that a symbiotic relationship with the natural world was necessary for survival. So, they taught respect and care for nature. When the Earth is ruined beyond repair, there will be no future for anything."

Olivia had a look on her face that Hannah had seen before, like she was considering this point of view. Even living in Ohio, they both had experienced massive storms and excessive heat. Climate change could not be ignored when it was pelting you with baseball-sized hail in the middle of spring. The entire world had been pulled into a partnership to mitigate the causes. Targeting greenhouse gas emissions to reduce global warming was a start. But she did not trust that corporations, with greedy people making the decisions, would take the steps needed. They would pay the fines and keep going.

Hannah took a breath and continued. "Based on our conversation before lunch, new methods might also rely heavily on science and innovation. Tell me, Olivia, what's going on at Ohio State that's new in the sciences?" Hannah sat in her favorite green leather chair, eagerly waiting for Olivia's response.

"I'm not really involved in that area, Hannah. Other members of my staff in Economic

Development look at grant applications for new research areas. What I remember is that research in physics, especially quantum physics, has been growing. Others are looking for new sources of energy. Then there is dark matter being researched in astrophysics. But I don't think you will find any children involved in areas like that," Olivia commented.

"You're right—probably not at that level. But children may be involved in a different way: through perceptual abilities. If you think about it, children are extremely perceptive early in life. They can coordinate massive amounts of information and learn at incredible speed. Some children carry this forward as they grow. They perceive patterns of behavior in people around them. And they understand where these patterns will lead.

"Here's one more adaptation I became aware of recently: physical changes. One young woman in Europe can darken her skin color to blend into the shadows of her environment, like a chameleon or an octopus. This adaptation is a change at the cellular level! But there is bound to be more out there than I know about right now." Hannah was breathless.

"And you believe that these children are the key to turning us back from the tipping point?" Olivia asked.

Hannah's eyes began to tear up. "I do. Think of what they could do if they worked together to solve a problem like water pollution. Blending their talents together, such as an environmental perspective, empathy, a physical adaptation, and a scientific breakthrough, they might find a way no one else could imagine."

"We would have to consider what their families would think about us taking their children away from their homes," Olivia said. "Could we ask some of the families to come live at the project site for a while?"

Hannah looked up at Olivia while two tears ran down the side of her face. "What's that look you are giving me?" Olivia was stunned. "Why are you crying?"

Hannah wiped away the tears. She giggled and grabbed Olivia's hands. "You said, 'We would have to consider ...' Does that mean what I think it means? Please tell me I'm not mistaken!"

Olivia abruptly sat down on the nearest chair, confirming without a word to Hannah that she did say that. "I think I need some alcohol, Hannah."

Hannah picked up her purse and car keys. "Me, too! Welcome to the project team, Olivia!"

Chapter 7: Maya and James Suweto

The next step was to start building the staff that would recruit, train, and nurture the children with extraordinary abilities. Hannah thought that Maya and James would be perfect for this task. She told Maya and her brother-in-law, James, about her unexpected windfall, begging them to keep the information to themselves until she determined what she wanted to do.

She asked them over for dinner on a Saturday night when it would be easier for them to find a sitter for the children. After they had polished off the spaghetti, meatballs, and Caesar salad, Hannah dumped the dishes in the sink, anxious to get started on her pitch to them.

"Maya, James, I finally have a plan for how to use the money. But the project I have in mind is really BIG, global in fact. I need all the help I can get to make it work. So, I would like both of you, and your children, to become involved. I know it's asking a lot of you. And there is no doubt that joining the project is going to turn your lives upside down. But I can guarantee the project will provide the best medical, educational, and support services you will ever need. Your salaries would be based on the responsibilities you decide to take on." Hannah took a breath and watched for their reaction.

Maya and James looked at each other and then back to Hannah.

James said, "We are family, but still before we make any commitments, we need to know, in great detail, exactly what this project is all about. Take your time. We're bound to have lots of questions." Maya nodded and motioned for Hannah to continue.

Hannah explained her concept of finding children with extraordinary talent, bringing them to a location where they could develop their skills, and eventually employing those talents to solve problems causing climate change and environment destruction. "If they could genetically pass those skills on, or teach them to others, it could radically change the development of the human race," Hannah said.

"Olivia and I spent the weekend defining the project structure. It won't be like a regular school or training camp. This is something new, and we will be feeling our way forward. Working together, the whole project can define new ways to help people, plants, animals, and the entire planet to survive. That is the primary mission. However, the main task at this point is the recruitment of qualified staff," Hannah said then thought, *Oh no! They look like I hit them on the head with a 2 x 4. Come on, Hannah. Break it down for them. Smaller pieces will be easier to handle.*

"I need a project team to hire teachers and mentors and to find families with exceptional children. I want to start with the mentors. We would advertise for young adults with new ideas for building a better world. They would look for and mentor children with special skills. As for teachers, they must be more willing to listen and learn from the children than teaching a previously established curriculum," Hannah explained.

"Now, how would you feel about Chelsea being part of this project?" Hannah continued. "She is a good example of the kinds of children this project is being built around. What questions would you ask as parents? Who do you want to mentor her? How do you think she would feel about being with other children with special talents, even when they're much different from her own?" Hannah knew that she had to be completely honest with them. *Still no comments or questions.*

"Come on, guys! How do you feel about this? Do you think you would be comfortable working in the recruitment effort? You could start that from your home here." Hannah could hear the desperation coming out in her voice. She wanted them to be with her so badly.

Maya responded with concern for her family that Hannah expected, based on her love and loyalty. "Chelsea and Bobby will be starting school in a few weeks. I don't think it's fair to take them away from their friends and childhood activities while they are so young. And coming from a military family, James was constantly forced to move around. Maybe we would be able to adapt to the changes. But I don't know whether we have enough expertise to do everything you need us to do. What do you think, James?"

"Hmmm ... I was right about having a lot of questions. I can think of ten right now! Where is this global project going to be located? We'll be separated from our families, friends, and our community here. I understand that there will be benefits for us. Maya and I will develop skills as we handle challenges that arise, and Bobby and Chelsea will have more resources to shape their futures. Choosing whether or not to be a part of this is probably the biggest decision we will ever make."

"I know how you feel, James. It's turned my life upside down already. It's up to good people like us to step up now. This money gives us a chance. The plan is gaining momentum. And whether we are ready or not, I have to move forward. The idea both scares and thrills me," Hannah said.

"Hannah, we need to talk to Bobby and Chelsea. Can you really walk away from Grams and Grandpa Neil? We need to think this through for at least a week." Maya was already looking ahead.

The longer they take to decide, the harder it will be for them to change.

"Unfortunately, the project and the funds are under time limit constraints. To be honest, I want you both to start right away," Hannah explained. "Please talk with Grams and Grandpa. They helped me to find a purpose for this money—a purpose that will mean something for our future."

Hannah gave Maya an especially long hug at the doorway as they were preparing to leave. Maya had tears in her eyes as the hug ended. "You couldn't just build a better mouse trap, could you?" she said.

Hannah laughed and waved goodbye as they got into their car.

Finally, after four days of Hannah's persuasive calls, Maya and James agreed to give this new experiment a six-month trial period. They would remain in their Ohio home, where the children would attend the same schools, and James and Maya would work on recruitment. They told Hannah that after six months, if they were asked to move, they would have to reconsider being involved with the project. If it wasn't working out for them, they would remain in Ohio. *At least there is a chance that they will want to stay with the project. After recruitment slows down, I'll ask them to participate in the project site determination. There might be some travel, but they can go back to their home.*

Chapter 8: Management Team Meeting

At Stephen's suggestion, Olivia volunteered to coordinate a meeting of the Finance and Management Teams from her home computer. She was no stranger to long-distance teleconferences after many years in the Economic Development Department at Ohio State University. Olivia was looking forward to meeting everyone and listening to their perspectives about the project.

Stephen signed on first at 5:50 a.m. "Hello, Olivia. Thanks for finding a time that works for everyone. I appreciate your quick response to my request. In order to get Hannah's project moving, we must have a strong Finance Team that understands their responsibilities. Did you receive the job descriptions I sent yesterday?"

Olivia first noticed Stephen's wavy, salt-and-pepper hair. She guessed he was between fifty and fifty-five. He wore round glasses with black frames, and had laugh lines around his eyes. "Nice to finally meet you, Stephen. Yes, the job descriptions are in and have been sent to the team. When are we going to set up a secure website?" Olivia asked.

"Soon. I agree that will be an effective way for us to communicate and keep our information confidential. But I reiterate, no spending without having the proper checks and balances in place. That's why we're having this meeting."

Hannah signed on next, waving to them both with her left hand while her right hand covered a huge yawn. "Oh my! Excuse me. I never seem to get enough sleep these days. Stephen, I'm expecting you to handle the review of the Finance Team's job descriptions and answer any questions. So, we're just waiting for Nicholai now?"

Olivia nodded. "In his email, he said he might be a few minutes late. Oh … he's signing in now. Welcome, Nicholai!"

"Hello, everyone. Hannah, it's so nice to see you again. And you must be Olivia," Nicholai said with a quick wink.

Olivia immediately noticed his high cheekbones and deep-set blue eyes. *Wow! What a hunk!* His broad shoulders were covered by an expensive-looking light blue sweater. *Back to business, girl.* "Stephen, please get us started."

"Here is the way I see us dividing up the financial responsibilities: Nicholai will have general oversight of the funds. He has an excellent record for managing large projects on budget. Also, he keeps the big picture in mind. Sometimes spending more for quality is important to the overall goal."

Nicholai started chuckling and said, "Stephen, I think I'll hire you to write my obituary! You are too kind. I will do my best for Hannah and the project. The sooner we start, the better off we'll be."

Stephen nodded, then continued, "Next, I'll take on the responsibility of investing part of the funds to create a steady income. This can be used to supplement certain expenses as needed. I'll also be responsible for creating the employment contracts and the land purchase, construction, and other legal documents, with assistance from Hannah's legal firm of Jackson, Montgomery, and Sheffield. I will also be the liaison with government officials. Are there any questions?"

"That sounds good to me," Hannah said. "I hope you're not overwhelmed with so many responsibilities on your shoulders. I know you wanted to use Lei Chen on the Finance Team, but I really want him to supervise the Accelerators."

"That's why he will be joining us later," Stephen noted. "I expect that we'll all juggle some tasks as needed, depending on the workload. Let's return to nailing down our assignments if there are no questions."

This guy is all business. Should I hold my questions until later? Olivia thought as she pushed slowly away from the screen, making her face smaller and less noticeable by the two financial wizards on the team. But she knew her role was just as important as theirs.

"Olivia, your jobs will be to review the expenditure requests from staff, to develop bid specifications for general ongoing supplies, and to ensure that we are buying from vendors that support our cause to the fullest extent possible. This will take more of your time, but if you prepare bid specs with the qualities we are looking for, that will make it easier. There will be some expensive one-time purchases, for example, an electron microscope or a saltwater aquarium. You might end up working with the teaching staff on the specs for equipment. They'll provide you with information, but you'll be responsible for securing what they need." Stephen paused, waiting for her questions.

"I think I can handle it. But I can come to you with specific questions or problems as they come up, right?" Olivia tried hard to keep the anxiety out of her voice, but she thought her voice sounded shaky.

Hannah came to her rescue. "Of course, we'll all be there for each other. That's what a team is. If you aren't sure, take an extra day to think about it. Do more research. Ask for help! This project is a big commitment. But never forget what we're fighting for. I want people and the Earth to survive."

Stephen jumped back in. "Hannah, your job is to approve the expenditures so that the bank can disperse the funds. The bank will send you monthly financial statements. You will review them with Nicholai to make sure we're on track. If either of you see anything you don't recognize in those statements, you need to tell me at once. I have signature cards for you to complete and send to the bank. Two signatures will be needed for all expenditures. Anything else come to mind at this point?"

No questions were asked. It was almost time for the second half of the conference to begin, so Olivia took a deep breath and used her management experience to wrap things up, saying, "Let's talk about our next steps. As Stephen pointed out to me earlier, we can't start spending money until we get those signature cards and the job descriptions to the bank. Tomorrow, please. Nicholai, Stephen tells me that you have computer technology experience. We need to set up a secure website to make it easier for everyone to communicate. Please get a cost estimate to create that, and don't forget all the enhanced cybersecurity we'll need for the safety of the staff and children. We also need a salary schedule. Stephen, Hannah told me that you were waiting to get started on this. We need to lay out all the positions for the project, then put in the salary ranges. Recruitment should be starting within the next ten days. Depending on the global reach and how long the job posting advertisements run, the budget for that alone could run into the tens of thousands of dollars."

Olivia stopped talking when she saw that Lei Chen Xiao was requesting to enter the meeting. "It's time for the Management Team to join us. I think we're off to a good start. Anything else you want to add before I admit him to the call, Stephen, Hannah, Nicholai?"

Hannah said, "I'm excited for the rest of you to meet Lei Chen, and also joining us will be Maya and James Suweto. Let's admit them and get started."

Lei Chen had previously met both Hannah and Stephen. His jet black hair was sticking up in its normal disheveled state. His green-and-gray striped tie had a soy sauce stain on it that he hoped no one would notice. His square-framed glasses had a tendency to slip down his nose, and no amount of adjusting seemed to fix the problem. He had developed a healthy respect for Stephen's extensive knowledge of worldwide financial transactions and investing. Hannah remained a mystery to him. She was pleasant and good-looking, but she had a strange way of looking at the world. He admired her commitment to making changes that would improve human interaction with the world and its resources. This would be his first opportunity for meeting the rest of the Management Team.

"Please welcome Lei Chen Xiao and Maya and James Suweto," Olivia said. Hannah and the rest of the members on the Zoom call waved to the newcomers.

Hannah quickly made introductions. "Olivia Hutchins is our Chief Operating Officer." Olivia smiled and said a brief "Hello." "Stephen Goldfarb is in charge of investment, contracts, and other legal matters in association with our lawyers. And Nicholai Resenden is in charge of the overall project, including management of the funds. I will approve all requests for expenditures and generally stick my nose into everything else."

Everyone chuckled at that statement, although they had no doubt it was true.

"Lei Chen, Maya, and James will be responsible for recruiting and hiring the staff and identifying the children for the project. Lei Chen will also supervise the Accelerator team. Olivia and I will work with him to define their qualifications, but it's really their personal qualities that will make them stand out. Maya and James will work with Stephen to prepare job posting advertisements for the teaching staff and the project support staff. Their real challenge will be to scour the world looking for children with unique skills that enable them to closely connect to their physical environments, animals, and people. Are there any questions?" Hannah nodded to Lei Chen and pointed to Maya and James.

Lei Chen looked puzzled. "Hannah, what are the Accelerators supposed to do? How am I going to supervise them if we don't have specific goals or targets to reach?"

Hannah was quiet for several minutes.

"Did you hear me, Hannah?" Lei Chen asked. "I am happy to work with young adults and children. But supervising is a tough job when there are no guardrails." *I might not accept this job if she doesn't come up with some answers for me,* he thought.

Hannah took a deep breath and closed her eyes. When she opened them, there were shiny silver glints that seemed to pierce right through him. "I'm sorry, Lei Chen, to keep you waiting for an answer. We'll need more time to discuss the Accelerators as we move forward. For now, I hope to find young adults who are willing to explore the world in partnership with young children, helping to find new ways to coexist. They must be willing to adapt and change. Their goals will be to strengthen the skills the children already have and to encourage them to work together to solve problems. I understand your reservations. You were my first choice for this position because I *think* you can rise to the challenge. Am I wrong?"

This is not fair! My success will be dependent upon how well both the children and the

Accelerators do their tasks. "What happens when I find they're not meeting their goals? Am I being a bad supervisor? Or are they failing for other reasons? How will you determine this?" Lei Chen asked.

Nicholai had been quiet for some time, but he spoke up to address the questions from Lei Chen. "This is new territory for all of us. The most important thing is for us to work through it together. Your questions say that you think we'll judge you harshly. I won't, and I don't think the others here will either. You can count on me for help whenever you need it. I'm excited to see what these people can do."

"We are, too!" Maya said. "James and I have lots of ideas for recruitment. The wording we use will attract people and children who aren't afraid to be different. The focus on conservation and working to understand what is happening to our world will also be the basis of interview questions later." The curls in her blonde hair bounced around as she talked.

Their excitement was contagious. Lei Chen felt his shoulders relax as he pushed his glasses back up his nose. He realized this group had good qualifications for what they were trying to accomplish, and he wondered if his fears were due to the judgmental nature of his parents. *I think I must give them a chance. And I won't know if I can be successful unless I try. This could be the opportunity of a lifetime.*

Hannah decided that they had accomplished what was needed. "I want to thank everyone for participating in the meeting. Your assignments for the next few weeks will be specific and time sensitive. Watch your emails for links to our Cloud site. Good luck and see you next time."

$+\ +\ +$

The next day, Maya and James created the social media job posting ads for the teachers and staff. Once the English versions were approved, they had the advertisements translated into other languages.

"The recruitment campaign needs to hit social media internationally next week," James told Maya one morning. "Let's target young adults for the Accelerator team. According to Hannah, they are a critical part of the project."

"Their salaries will be attractive enough to reflect that," Maya noted.

"We need to attract people who are not afraid to use their intuition and perceptive abilities, who can accept children who are different and encourage them to develop in their own ways," James said, adding that text to the recruitment advertisements.

In the first three days of their social media campaign, Maya and James received more than 2,500 applications. Hannah sent them a bonus check for their hard work and quick success. Because Maya and James were overwhelmed with so many applications to process, Olivia stepped in to help, directing Maya and James to ask for recommendation letters to help decide which applicants to interview.

"Let's set up phone interviews with some of the candidates," Maya said. "We need to hear their voices. That will tell us more about each person than pieces of paper." Maya was determined to find the best people to invite for the interview process.

Chapter 9: The Accelerator Candidates

The Accelerators interview process started when Olivia and Lei Chen agreed to help Maya and James with the selections. Olivia had resigned her position at Ohio State after the fall semester final exams were completed. She began working full-time on the project just after the first of the year.

As they worked together, Maya was astonished at how each of them developed questions to assess different qualities. They seemed to complement each other's abilities naturally. Lei Chen worked to reveal the candidates' intellect and mentoring qualities, and Olivia investigated their social consciousness. James developed questions that would indicate whether a candidate had a cooperative or competitive nature. Maya worked from the perspective of a mother with an extraordinary child, as the final piece needed for the interview team. All candidates were asked the same questions.

One outstanding candidate was Tomas Ojeda, a young man from Guatemala with a unique perspective on how to reach children.

James asked him the first question. "How would you develop problem-solving ability in others?"

Tomas sat quietly, thinking out his answer to this question. His black hair fell across his hazel eyes as he brought his hands forward on the tabletop.

"I know you'll think this is strange, but putting puzzles together is a good start. It seems to me that problem-solving is looking at all of the little pieces that make up a whole. You have to see each piece, recognize its pattern, and see where it fits together with other pieces. What's really hard is when you *think you know* what the puzzle should look like, but it keeps changing. Life is like that: Just when you think you've solved the puzzle, it changes. You have to have the ability to keep working even when it looks like you've failed. Resolving problems is intrinsically rewarding. What do you do when the picture is not clear? Try a different perspective," Tomas said.

Lei Chen raised his eyebrows. *An original thinker.* "Have you ever had a special relationship with an animal?" Tomas nodded. "Please describe it for us."

Tomas looked at the panel members and smiled. "When I was five, a stray kitten climbed in through my bedroom window and slept with me. When I woke, she was curled up next to my side. I think my parents wanted me to learn about responsibility by taking care of her, so they let her stay. But she became far more to me than my parents expected. I named her Carina, and she filled up empty places inside that I didn't know were there. She was very playful, and I needed that because I was always so afraid. Fighting in Guatemala never seemed to stop. As Carina grew older, she became more independent. She explored our neighborhood, and so did I as I went looking for her. I started to make friends with other children who had cats, or dogs, or birds. She taught me that I had to go out and face what was out there. As I grew up, school became hard. When I felt defeated, she came to my room, sat on my schoolbooks, and purred. It was like she approved of the information and wanted me to feel joy as I learned it."

Tomas took a deep breath and continued. "Every time she did that, I would laugh. When I opened the books again, the words looked different, easier to understand. As time went on, I realized that I could feel her inside me, prompting me to try new things, to be brave, to find joy. When Carina had kittens, it provided another set of lessons for me. Now our family was bigger, and I learned there was enough love and joy to go around for all."

Time was up, and the panel needed to move to their next candidate. Maya thanked Tomas, letting him know decisions would be made within two weeks.

"Our next candidate, Amanda Collins, is from Australia," Maya announced.

Olivia stood and opened the door for Amanda. She was tall and willowy, reminding Olivia of a distance runner. Olivia said, "Please have a seat. This is Lei Chen Xiao and Maya and James Suweto. I am Olivia Hutchins. Would you like some water before we get started?"

"Oh, thank you! I am a little nervous but ready to get started," Amanda said.

"What is it like growing up in Australia?" Maya asked.

"Well, it's home. I loved to go outside and watch the animals and birds in the trees. We had eucalyptus trees along the east side of our property. Koalas love eucalyptus leaves, so they were always around. Mostly it was dry and hot. We had two really bad fires. When they burn through grasslands, the wildlife stampede and fly out, taking shelter wherever there is water. Everyone pitches in to stop the fire from spreading, digging trenches or spraying foam. My parents taught me to respect the land. I watched as the climate grew hotter, and the animals suffered or moved away. Our family joined a conservation group, so we all learned more about the island. It was really amazing when we went out to the coast. The sea, the ocean plants, and the fish—an entirely different ecosystem. I'm still learning, but there is a lot to love about Australia," Amanda noted with pride.

Olivia presented the next question. "Why is it important to face your fears?"

"You will never know what you can accomplish unless you work your way through your fears. Everyone feels fear. It's a natural response to danger. And danger can come from anywhere. You fight against it by preparing. The first one I faced was failure. What happens when you fail? I ask myself what I learned from the attempt and what I would do differently the next time. The more I try, the less afraid I usually feel. Both success and failure play key roles in learning. The most important people in my life made me feel as though I could tackle anything. I only needed to keep going."

When the interview concluded and Amanda had left the room, Maya said, "I think she will be a good team member. Hannah told me that flexibility and determination are skills that we all need for the project to succeed."

The next candidate was interviewed via Zoom. He was a sturdily built young man from Ireland with curly red hair named Logan McIntyre. Olivia had a difficult question for him and was eager to see what he would say. "Hello, Logan. What qualities are needed for leadership?"

Logan smiled, "Not afraid to ask the tough questions, are you? My studies show the people who desperately want to lead have the most disastrous effect on the world. They are often people with charisma, but that usually masks underlying deficiencies that show up when things get tough. When I was growing up in Ireland, the violence and struggles for leadership proved to be bad for everyone. Ironically, it's the people who don't want to lead, but have qualities that others trust and value, who should be in positions of leadership. Those people seek cooperation as the likely road to success. They bring out the best in others. They are good listeners. They wrestle with problems, break them down, figure them out, and find a way forward. They don't run away when things get rough or complicated. And, what I really admire is they have the ability to *change direction* based on the facts."

James posed the next question. "What is the worst problem affecting the world today?"

"I wish I had a more global perspective, but I imagine that the problems are the same everywhere. Greed? Shortsightedness? Lack of accountability? I guess those are my top three. The worst of it is that good people, people who really care about their communities, their environment, and the world, don't have enough power. They need money to combat the awful things that are being done, and they need something even more powerful than money to change the way things are done. I just wish I knew what that something was. But I'll keep trying to find it. That's what this project is all about, isn't it?"

James was quick to respond. "That is perceptive of you. Yes, we are looking for people to help change the way things are being done. But more importantly, we are running out of time to do it."

Logan gulped and nodded.

The last interview of the day was a Zoom conference with a young woman from South Africa. M'gera Kumalo was strong and accomplished. Her application showed her to be fiercely independent. Olivia wondered if she would be comfortable in a closely connected team.

Lei Chen started the teleconference with her. "Good afternoon and thank you for applying to be part of this project. Here is your first question: When is a team more valuable than an individual for achieving the best outcome?"

M'gera's hair was tightly braided against her head. When she smiled, her big white teeth stood out against her black skin. Her voice was soft as she answered. "When? Every tick of the clock produces a different when. One person may have the best ability to handle the situation now, but someone else may be best in the next moment. A team with combined strengths has more resources to use as changes happen. A team also can overcome weaknesses in individuals by working together. But teams need time to develop trust. Eventually, that trust creates a bond between people and leads to greater achievements, especially when there is danger."

Olivia leaned in and asked, "Please describe the most important moment in your life so far."

M'gera breathed deeply; her eyes glittered when she looked at Olivia. "When I was ten years old, I was hiking in the mountains with my father and brothers. We became separated when a flash flood destroyed the path we were on. I called out to them, but no one answered. As I sat there in the rain, I was afraid they had been washed out of my life, completely taken away. I felt so alone and afraid. After a while, I felt the mountain under me pouring its strength into my body. The rain fell gently on my hair, caressing my face as it ran down to the ground. My senses opened up completely. I heard birds chirping in the trees. I smelled the herbs that grew on the side of the ravine. My heart stopped pounding, and peace flowed through me. I became connected to the Earth as a vital part of my being. A few hours later, my father found me. Everyone was okay. But I had been changed forever."

Chapter 10: Gustav von Telleman

A Professor of chemistry at Heidelberg University in Germany, Gustav von Telleman had recently completed development of a powerful neurotoxin. It was colorless, odorless, and tasteless and distilled from various animal and vegetable compounds over several years of experimentation. When he wanted to test it, he went to the forest near where he grew up. He trapped a rabbit, administered the neurotoxin, and watched its effects. Its back muscles twitched, spasmed, and then went flaccid. The pink around its eyes gradually became redder as the tiny blood vessels burst. Saliva oozed out of its mouth. Traces of foam near the gum line were remnants of teeth after they dissolved. *Extremely effective,* Gustav thought. *And also untraceable.*

Gustav knew that his penchant for inflicting pain came from his domineering, abusive father. To survive his childhood, he was forced to hide his emotional responses. Having felt so violated growing up, he craved situations where he was in control. After confirming the test subject was dead, he used the shovel he had brought to the woods for digging a firepit into the forest floor, then he lined it with stones blackened from other nearby campsites. He put the remains of the rabbit into the fire, adding boughs of dead pine and dried-out cones to build the flames. He lit a match, tossing it into the pit. As Gustav contemplated the fire, a hazy memory swam to the surface in wispy snatches of light.

Eight years old, alone in his upstairs bedroom, strange noises created weird, twisting nightmares. He ran downstairs, crying and carrying his blanket, to his parents' bedroom door. He knocked tentatively. "Papa, Mama, are you awake?" he cried. He heard muffled voices from the room. Then his father, Heinrich von Telleman, stood framed between the doorposts, backlit by the flames from the fireplace inside.

"Why are you crying, Gustav?" his father had said.

"I'm afraid of the dark," Gustav confessed.

His father's piercing, blue-grey eyes scanned him from head to toe, as if he were a cockroach that had suddenly appeared from under the floorboards. "You are not a baby to be pampered and protected. You are a young man. Get the tent from the closet under the stairs. You will sleep outside for the next five nights, until you are no longer afraid. No fires, no lights. Go, and do not return until daylight hits the porch from above the trees."

"No, Heinrich!" his mother had protested.

His father walked back to the bed and slapped her face hard, leaving a red handprint on her cheek. She hid under the blankets, whimpering.

Gustav went to the closet, quickly finding the tent, then set it up, and crawled inside with his blanket. The only sounds he heard came from the wind in the trees and small animal feet scampering on the pine needles. He got no sleep for the first two nights. But gradually, he learned what the noises meant. He began to understand the pattern of life there, the cycles of day and night. That made sense to him in a way that his parents' behavior never would.

As the memory slowly dissolved, Gustav returned his attention to the firepit. The neurotoxin compound was safely enclosed inside bubble wrap in his backpack. He burned leaves with remnants of the toxin in the pit with the rabbit carcass. There was nothing to identify who had been there: He was just another hiker passing through, using the firepit to keep away the darkness.

Gustav needed time to reset his emotions. He found that maintaining a cold numbness as his general emotional state served him well in his interactions with other people. When he thought about himself, he pictured a black void with a huge, slowly swirling vortex at its center. The dynamic, violent forces of nature called to that black void within him. *Such power.*

His job at the University had served his purposes well over the past five years. He had abundant resources at his fingertips, including the oldest and one of the largest libraries in all of Germany. He was familiar and comfortable with the climate—cold in fall and winter and mild in spring and summer. His schedule enabled him to escape into the mountains or the countryside for intellectual pursuits or to indulge his solitary nature. When he joined the University staff, people had been curious to find out what was underneath his mysterious, quiet exterior. He was tall, six feet three inches, and well-muscled and tan from his excursions in the mountains, with sandy blond hair and ice-blue eyes.

He had been working with Brandt Pharmaceuticals, a private company that sponsored many research projects at the University. His latest experiments with neurotoxin combinations could be very lucrative for drug companies in combination with other substances. Within a few months, he would start a bidding war. The deeper he became involved in business negotiations, the more predictable the outcomes became. There were fewer challenges along this road and not much to capture his interest. It was time for him to see what else was out there.

Gustav came across a recruitment for a child development project one day when he was scanning the message board at the University. They were looking for teaching staff that would be willing to work with children of all ages and backgrounds to stimulate their abilities in engineering, science, environmental research, and perception. *This might be promising,* Gustav thought. *The benefits look like the change would be worth it. Not that I like children, but they are so easy to manipulate.* Gustav took a picture of the bulletin with his phone.

Upon reaching his apartment in town, he pulled up an old resume and updated the information on his accomplishments, published papers on chemical compounds, and current experiments. The cover letter would be tricky. He needed to learn more about the project to make the letter into an impressive marketing piece. He couldn't find any other information on the project through the internet, so he decided to call some of his European colleagues to see if they knew anything about it.

A few days later, he got an email from one of his former laboratory assistants. She had applied for a position with the project and received an email from Olivia Hutchins. She gave Gustav Olivia's email address and wished him luck. Gustav emailed his updated resume and a list of questions to Olivia.

When Olivia received Gustav's email, she carefully scanned it, along with applications from other potential teaching staff. This selection process was so much different than the process for the Accelerator group. Mostly, the teaching candidates wanted to know the class size, salary range, and job location. They had received some very outstanding applications from candidates who were eager to develop their fields with young people to inspire them. The Finance Team quickly negotiated salaries with them, explaining that they were in the process of securing the project site and would provide more information later.

While Olivia was impressed by Gustav's resume, she felt his questions were unusual. His credentials were impeccable, but Olivia couldn't get a handle on him as a *person*. She decided to seek more information about him from his superiors, coworkers, and undergraduate staff. They frequently said that, "He is a very private person," or "He handles his duties at the University effectively and has made significant contributions to the field of chemistry." Strange comments. Olivia suspected they were either restricted in what they could tell her, or they didn't really know him at all.

Gustav's questions in his email showed that he wanted to know more about the project goals, which was normal. But his other questions weren't relevant to teaching children. He asked, "How much management oversight will there be of my classes? Chemistry curriculum is standard for most educational institutions. No further development should be needed."

Then he asked, "How much time will be available for me to continue my private business interests?" That question told Olivia that he had problems with authority figures. His expertise was undoubtedly needed to round out the teaching staff. But in her gut, she felt that something was wrong.

Chapter 11: Lei Chen Meets the Accelerators

Lei Chen ushered the Accelerators into the conference room. He shook their hands and motioned them to take seats. He looked like he hadn't slept for days. His broadcloth shirt was wrinkled, his sport coat had papers sticking out of the pockets, and his black hair was combed on the left side, but not on the right.

"Good morning, and thank you for getting here so quickly. David Kamatsu could not be with us today, but he will also be a member of the Accelerator team."

Logan McIntyre, Teani Horikawa, Amanda Collins, M'gera Kumalo, and Tomas Ojeda seated themselves around the table. All showed enhanced qualities of empathy, insight, focused intensity, and great communication ability. He expected that their competitive natures might show up later. But for now, their individual skills would be needed to recruit the children. The Accelerators activated their computer tablets and pulled up the project timeline.

Logan cleared his throat and raised his hand. Lei Chen blinked, but nodded for Logan to ask his question.

"Why are we called 'Accelerators'? Are we supposed to make things happen more rapidly?"

"That's a good question. Let me see if I can explain it. The title is for your overall function of developing better human beings. When you meet the children, you will understand more. The Accelerators create Challenges that will spur the children on to reach the potential of their gifts. These Challenges will also teach them how to work together with their skills to solve problems."

Tomas nodded. "Yes, we are in the middle between the children and the outside world. To help them ... what's the word? *Navegar?*"

"To navigate," Lei Chen translated for the group. "I am giving each of you a list of five to seven children, ages four to fourteen, to meet and evaluate for the project. You will need to assess their abilities, talk with their parents or guardians and teachers, and use your own skills to encourage them to work with us. You will have four months to make your visits and submit your final recommendations. I will be coordinating your travel assignments, translators if needed, and finances. I will also be available to talk with the families and the children, if you believe it would be helpful. You have been given some information that the interview teams received from the adults around the children. Do you have any questions at this point?"

Teani looked at him with her golden eyes. "I have a question about Emilio Ricci. He looks like a great candidate. But I don't know whether I would be the best person to evaluate his skills. His areas of interest are science, geography, and the atmosphere. I am not a very scientific person. Why was he assigned to me?"

Lei Chen smiled. "You were selected to talk to him at this stage because he is so unsure of himself. No one in his family understands what he is doing. He takes in information like water. After he thinks about it, his questions are so advanced that his teachers need to research the answers to talk with him. Emilio needs a guiding light, someone who will help him believe in himself. Your openness will let him go in new directions, where others would channel him into already known paths. Do you see what I mean?"

She sighed. "Yes, thank you for explaining. I can see it now."

Amanda raised her hand. Lei Chen nodded for her to continue. "Tamlyn's information is very sketchy, inconsistent. I don't know what to make of it. She's older than the other children, almost my age. She might be very uncomfortable trying to fit in. She is in Austria. It might be better for me to work with children in South America, Australia, and New Zealand. Can we move some of the candidates between us?"

"There are reasons you were paired with the candidates you were given, like Teani and Emilio. We do not have time to go over the reasons now. You must do the best you can. We will be in touch during your travels through the Team website. Are there any other questions?" Lei Chen was anxious for them to get started.

Logan said, "We don't really know how this process will pan out. Could we consult with each other during the process? I know that time is short, but we might actually save time by working together."

Lei Chen considered this suggestion. It might be a good way to cement the team, or it could provoke a lot of arguments. "I want you to check in with me first before you consult with each other. I may have more information that will help you to move forward. And I want you to remember this: The Accelerator team is critical to the project's success. You must build trust in me, in each other, and in yourselves. This will take time and patience. Do you understand?"

They looked at each other, then at Lei Chen. They nodded or said "Yes" to his question.

Then M'gera said, "It will feel strange to be in new places for me. I often need a day to orient to the new environment before I talk to people."

"You all have the skills you need to connect with people. Learn what you can from them. Answer their questions. Look at their lives. The youngest children may not be ready to leave their families. There will be opportunities for them in future years." Lei Chen moved to the door and opened it.

Teani pulled him to the side after the other Accelerators had left the conference room. "Excuse me, Mr. Xiao. You look a little ruffled. As the preeminent Empath in the group, I suggest that you spend an hour in a hot tub followed by a massage. I also suggest that you keep a change of clothes with you, just in case a parent video conference is requested at the last minute. You're not just a paper pusher. We do want to make a good impression, don't we?" she said with a twinkle in her eyes.

He was stunned. "Please call me Lei Chen. Thank you for the suggestions. I am terrible about taking care of myself when I am focused on getting things done. I hope that you will take care of each other as well as you are trying to take care of me!" Lei Chen patted her on the shoulder and escorted her out to the elevators.

Logan, Tomas, M'gera, and Amanda wondered what had happened to Teani. "Maybe she had some personal questions that she didn't want to bring up in front of us," Tomas said.

"I'm trying to imagine what it will be like, meeting these special children, but I really can't. There's a lot of pressure on us," Logan said.

Amanda nodded. "I feel it, too. But I am dying to meet these children and their families. What an adventure!"

Teani joined the group as the elevator doors opened. They piled in together, smiling and putting their arms on each other's shoulders.

Chapter 12: The Project Site Search

With recruitment for the teaching staff, Accelerators, and special children well underway, the Finance Team now focused on finding a project site. At a planning conference call, Hannah requested they search for ten square miles of land that offered natural water collection areas, forested mountains, and flatland for building construction, a combination that would not be easy to find. They didn't want the site to be isolated from surrounding communities, but they realized that the amount of land would automatically create space for privacy.

The project would need the support of government and local leaders, requiring tough negotiation and sensitivity to current issues. Olivia determined that political stability for at least the past 100 to 200 years was needed to protect the project from physical danger. When Hannah approved that criterion, it eliminated the Middle East, Russia, China, and Somalia as well as countries bordering them. Political divisiveness in the United States, especially where children were concerned, eliminated it from consideration as a project site. Access to medical facilities, transportation, and communication resources were the other defining considerations.

"What about climate?" Nicholai asked. "Temperate areas are more densely populated, and the cost of land will be much higher."

"Our definition for the land needs will eliminate areas of extreme and unpredictable weather patterns," Hannah noted. "So where does that leave us, Stephen?"

"Southern parts of Canada, Argentina, South Australia, New Zealand, Spain, and France," he replied. "With a little more research, especially in the area of governmental support, I think we can narrow it down. We're going to need to access more project funds to negotiate for the purchase of the project site. Hannah, are there any restrictions from the lawyers we need to know about before we start?"

"I don't know. There is nothing in the contracts I signed with them about their power to influence our decisions. How much money will we need to buy the site?" Hannah asked.

"$500 million to $1 billion for the project site. Based on market rates, after four to five months, the price will go up by 10 to 15 percent. We will be bidding against developers who are working to acquire land for commercial expansion," Nicholai said, looking at his notes.

Compared to $60 billion, that was a small amount. But it was more money than Hannah had ever had control of in her life. *What if I make the wrong decision? If I pick the wrong site, will there be enough time to start again?* Hannah shook her head, noticing the questioning look on Olivia's face.

"Nicholai, if you can prepare a report on land costs in the areas Stephen listed, then I can get the lawyers to release the funds. I don't know how much time we have, but we need to push hard on the site selection. We need the money on hand as leverage to use for negotiation. Let's meet again at this same time tomorrow." Hannah closed the meeting.

Next, she called Dirk Jackson, starting the conversation with the finance questions. However, the finance discussion was cut short when Dirk relayed some startling information. Hannah's benefactor had left instructions with the lawyers for when the project idea had been crystallized.

"You will have twenty-four months from now and 15 percent of the funds from the endowment to start testing your theory to see if it will produce results," Dirk said.

That's more than enough money, based on the information from Nicholai. But twenty-four months! Is that possible? She started to choke up.

"Dirk, you can't be serious! We probably need a full year just to negotiate the purchase of the site. And then it will take another two years to get it built. What can we do to get an extension?" Hannah was desperate.

"Hannah, we can't change the terms laid out for us. You have your instructions, and we have ours. I'll make the money available for your use by the end of the day. We can also offer our services to set up the site purchase contract. You should have enough money available to hire a real estate development company to investigate sites and make recommendations for you. That will save you some time," Dirk suggested.

Hannah was silent for a full minute, thinking through the restrictions and options. "I guess I need to figure this out. I'll bring it back to my Finance Team and let you know if I need anything else from you. Wish me luck!"

The new timeline created pressure for everyone involved.

When Hannah returned to her condominium, she found another letter from Denver in her mailbox.

Dear Hannah,

I am impressed by the work you have started to help save the Earth. The lawyers have informed you about the first deadline that they are required to enforce. I told you that time is running out. Deadlines will help you to keep that in mind. The location where the changes will begin is critical to the project's success. Choose with your heart as well as with the data collected by your team. There will be many obstacles in your way before there is a solid road to follow. Remember, I believe in you.

Your friend and benefactor

The letter was a surprise. Hannah felt that her benefactor was secretly looking over her shoulder, cheering her on. *Who is it? It must be someone I knew in school. I just don't have time to find him or her now.*

Over the next two weeks, the Finance Team determined Argentina, Spain, and France to be unsuitable due to difficulty working with the governments. The sparse rainfall and lack of forested area removed Australia from consideration. They were left with British Columbia in Canada and New Zealand. Both areas had plenty of land that met all of Hannah's criteria. She also thought that the neighboring communities would be sympathetic with the project goals.

I just keep going over and over the same information. How am I going to make a decision? Do I really need to visit the potential sites? Actually, I think I do. Maya and Stephen can come with me to New Zealand first. We can collect impressions of what the country is like. That will tell us more than words on paper, and pictures about places we've never visited. We need to talk to people. That's the missing piece.

Hannah picked up the phone to call Stephen and then realized that it was two o'clock in the morning in London. She decided to send him an email instead.

Stephen, please make travel arrangements for a trip to New Zealand for you, me, and Maya. Let's fly into the Queenstown airport. The property we selected is north of there. Contact me when you wake up, and we can go over the details. Thanks!

Hannah breathed a sigh of relief. *No time to waste.*

Chapter 13: Trip to New Zealand

Hannah divided the workload for the next couple of days to feel out the New Zealand potential project site. Maya would find a guide to take her to the site the first day for a tour and to take pictures. Stephen would check out the transportation, communication, and medical systems around the Queenstown area. Hannah would meet with local leaders to see New Zealand through their eyes.

After their flight arrived in Queenstown, Hannah opted to rent a car to take her from Queenstown to Dunedin. It was early spring with fragrant breezes blowing as she drove south. Through his banking contacts, Stephen arranged for Hannah to meet a former member of the New Zealand government. Sarah Marie Dowie had been a cabinet member from 2014 through 2020, and Hannah was hoping to get inside perspectives from her. Plus, she knew that a governmental liaison would be critical for their final negotiations.

When Hannah lifted the door knocker on Sarah's charming, two-story house, she heard footsteps approaching. Sarah opened the door and smiled. Her long blonde hair and green eyes reminded Hannah of Grams when she was younger.

"Come in," Sarah said, inviting Hannah into a comfortable sitting room, where a vase filled with colorful flowers sat on the table between two blue-

and-white armchairs. "Would you like some coffee or tea?"

"Actually, water would be fine," Hannah responded. She accepted the glass Sarah set beside her on the table. The water was cool and refreshing after the long drive. "This is the first time I've been to New Zealand. I read about the country on the internet and saw many pictures of the two islands. But you can't get a feeling for its character from those things. I want to see it through the eyes of the people who live here. I am looking for a place to start a project we are developing. So, if you don't mind, I want to ask about your experience in government here, as well as your perspective on where this country is going."

"I happen to agree with your point of view," Sarah told her. "I'm happy to share my perspectives and hope they will prove helpful to you. The years when I held office here were exciting, challenging, and fulfilling. I was lucky to be able to work with seasoned politicians as well as newcomers with high ideals. During those years, the legislature worked primarily on trade agreements, improving public education, and increasing sustainable energy sources. Public participation in the electoral process was eighty-four-and-a-half percent last year. We are very proud of that. What I'm hoping for now is to see more women in the legislature. A balanced viewpoint is increasingly important for the future of New Zealand."

Hannah felt like Sarah was reciting a political speech. She decided to confront her with that to see how she would respond. "Sarah, I'm familiar with how politicians address the public. Maybe I'm asking the wrong questions. Let's try this: Tell me three bad things about this country and three good things. And please, be honest with me. I really want to know."

Sarah looked into Hannah's eyes and sighed. "It's hard to break away from the way information is relayed in politics. I'm sorry. Let me think for a minute ... three bad things. First, illegal drug traffic has been steadily climbing, and we can't seem to get a grip on it. Second, this country has been largely agricultural for a long time. Moving the population toward higher education and advanced technology is like climbing uphill with a heavy truck on your back. Finally, the cost of medicine is still too high. Truly affordable nationwide health care seems like it should be a top priority, but it's not."

Hannah nodded. "Thanks for that. Seems like all democratically run countries are facing the same problems. Now, how about the good things? Your personal experience, please."

"Okay, fair enough. I learned a lot about the native tribes during my time serving the South Island. They have lived on these islands for thousands of years. They are resourceful, they treasure the Earth, and they hold tightly to family as a source of strength. Next, New Zealand is a varied and beautiful country, with mountains, oceans, lakes, and lush valleys. I genuinely love this place. And last, we expected that the global pandemic would shut New Zealand down. It actually had the opposite effect. There was unanimous support for vaccines, quick adoption of procedures to reduce the spread, and people stepping up to help their neighbors."

Sarah continued. "I understand that you are sponsoring a large project and are looking for a base of operations."

Now how did she hear about that? I thought we had kept the lid on this fairly well so far. "Pardon me, but how did you know about our project?"

"You can't be part of a country's government without frequently gathering intelligence," Sarah said. "We use the internet, of course. We've seen your recruitment going on for almost a year. And I also have sources of my own. Could you tell me anything more about the project? I have developed certain theories based on the recruitment advertisements, and I would like to know more about it."

Hannah wasn't sure how much information she should share with this stranger. But she needed to know if Sarah would be supportive of the idea. "We would like to build a facility for children with extraordinary talents or skills. The purpose of this facility is to encourage the development of their special characteristics and to study them scientifically with respect to genetic transmissibility and evolutionary potential. Our worldwide studies have shown us that there are amazing children everywhere, in some places where there is no support for them or their families. Their talents cover a very wide range, from musical genius to the ability to communicate with animals. We think that these special skills are needed right now to help solve problems, and they will be critical for the future development of the world. I could go on and on about it, but let me slow down to see if you have other questions I can answer."

"Are you recruiting children from New Zealand? Some children in the Maori tribe can create medicines from native plants that have proven very effective to treat ailments and injuries," Sarah said. "The native Indian populations in North America have similar traditions, or so the research I've done indicates."

Hannah was surprised at how quickly Sarah caught on to the idea. "We would be happy to get any referrals from you for children and also for teachers, mentors, specialists, and administrators. The facility will be fairly large. We are looking for about ten square kilometers. We will start with about fifty children and grow from there."

Sarah was quiet for a few minutes while Hannah finished drinking her water. Then she retrieved a book from one of the shelves in her sitting room.

"I'm going to highlight the names of some people who I think can help you. And you can call me at this number if you need more assistance," Sarah said, handing Hannah her card. "However, they will all be asking the same question: *What's in it for them?*"

At least she isn't shy about bringing that into the conversation, Hannah thought. "Yes, this will have to be a mutually beneficial relationship. It will take time for us to learn how things are done here and to build a platform for mutual understanding. Would you be willing to act as a liaison between the project and the government of New Zealand? Or if you aren't available, maybe you could refer me to someone else?"

Sarah tilted her head to one side, twisting a strand of her hair around her finger. Hannah worried that she might be pushing her too hard. But Sarah was exactly the kind of person she wanted to be involved at this point as she decided whether or not to build the project in New Zealand.

"Please consider this request," Hannah urged. "We could probably meet your salary requirements, and it would not be a long-term job, unless you wanted to remain with the project."

"I need to discuss it with my husband and my daughter," Sarah said. "I will let you know in a few days. I realize it is an important decision for the project. But you have certainly captured my interest."

Hannah picked up the book along with Sarah's card. "Thank you for taking the time to talk with me today and for your honesty. I look forward to hearing from you soon."

Chapter 14: The Project Site Selection

"I think the project site within the forested area in New Zealand would be perfect," Maya told Hannah. She had taken lots of pictures and was uploading them to the website. Maya's guide knew a lot about the area, showing her the lakes and streams and some of the animals and plants. The mountains and chasms would be challenging for the athletic children and the Accelerators. Current access was via jeep on a dirt road, so paved roads would be needed from the north and the west into the site. With the lack of cell and internet service, they would be starting from scratch there.

Hannah and Maya had discussed moving the whole family with the project. Chelsea had been recruited due to her musical talent. She had grown considerably more outgoing in the past two years since Hannah had decided to take on the human evolution project, which she had named XL-ENCE, because the challenge was larger than life. Grams and Grandpa Neil had stepped up to help support the family. It was hard on them with Maya and Hannah being away so much. Getting the project started colored Hannah's waking and sleeping thoughts.

"Listen, folks," Hannah said, tapping her foot impatiently as she addressed the Management Team on Zoom from her condo back in Ohio. "We're running out of time. New Zealand has so much potential for us as the project site. If we have to shift gears and visit the potential site in British Columbia, we won't make the deadline." *Sixty billion dollars is slipping away before my eyes. I can't let that happen. All the pieces are here. We just have to act.* "I will make this decision alone, but I was honestly hoping for more support from the rest of you."

Stephen spoke up first. "The Prince George area in British Columbia is still a viable alternative. We don't have the details of the site purchase cost back yet. Is there another reason why we are not considering that option?"

"Three factors impact the decision to develop the project there," James answered. "First, the economic base relies heavily on deforestation and mining. Although the province is moving rapidly to increase tourism, many attractions center on the beauty of the natural landscape. The deforestation and mining will cause more damage that becomes harder to reverse with time. Second, British Columbia is fighting for greater representation in the Canadian government. This battle has become more heated during the past ten years, leading to greater splintering of the political parties there. And third, health care, especially the opioid crisis, is the number one concern of its citizens. The environment is way down on their list, although that is the main focus for the use of the funds for our project. How many fronts do we want to fight on for success?" James was at his best, summing up the issues for the team.

Hannah nodded to James and addressed the team again. "I know that we won't find a perfect place to build the project. New Zealand is the best choice we have right now. Are there any objections?"

Olivia and Nicholai looked at each other and shrugged. Olivia spoke up first. "Hannah, we *are* supporting you. But the paperwork is formidable. The lawyers are pushing back and slowing us down, nitpicking at every turn. We are ready to start on construction plans for the site, but we can't prepare anything realistic until the land is under contract."

"Hannah," Nicholai spoke to bring other areas into focus. "You said that you might have a local politician who could help us. We could use someone like that right now. Sarah Dowie, I think you said her name was? What will it take to convince her?"

"She hasn't called back, but I'll get in touch with her again. It's time to start using that money to turn things our way."

Later that day, Hannah contacted Sarah again, begging for her assistance. "Good morning, Sarah. I wanted to update you on our progress. Our Chief Financial Officer, Stephen Goldfarb, is trying hard to work with government officials to coordinate everything that needs to be done. We could really use your help now. Do you have time to meet with us to figure this out?"

"Hello, Hannah. What have you offered them to get their cooperation? I'm sure you recall my warning about 'quid pro quo.' I suggest that you look closer at what's happening in Queenstown. You'll be interacting with them as your closest neighbors. What do they need?"

Of course! Politics as usual. "Thank you, Sarah. Sometimes I get too caught up in the details to remember the big picture. I'm sure we can find lots of ways to help."

After Hannah shared this information with the Management Team, Nicholai, working with Sarah, developed ways to invest the project funds into the local economy that fit with their goals. It made more sense to purchase the specific equipment to study astronomy, oceanography, medicine, and ecology and install them at local facilities. Those facilities would be expanded to incorporate new branches of study that the project and its students would need. Sarah helped Nicholai develop a contract template to obtain consent of the participating institutions and present the contracts to government officials to secure their cooperation.

Hannah, Stephen, and Nicholai spent hours updating the financial projections to incorporate the new agreements. They were getting close to the $4 billion mark.

"Look, Hannah," Stephen said. "These expenditures are reasonable at this stage of the project. Also remember that we are amassing a substantial amount of interest from the banks, 6½ percent as of the last statement. This gives us some leeway in our negotiations. The bloody lawyers reviewed the contracts we developed with Sarah's assistance, and even they couldn't find any holes."

"Let's get those contracts signed, gentlemen. We have four weeks based on the deadline. We need to give everyone time to wrap up their lives at home and move to New Zealand. We must get the project site built during the spring, summer, and early fall. Time is short, and we can't ask people to work and sleep in tents!"

"We're with you, Hannah. Let's post the info on the website," Nicholai suggested. "There are bound to be places where we can stay during the construction. I'll call Sarah to see what she can arrange for us."

"Thank you, Nicholai. See you both very soon." Hannah signed off and started listing the things she had to finish before moving.

+ + +

When the time came to move to New Zealand, Maya and James flew Grams and Grandpa Larsen into Columbus, Ohio, so they could have a few days together with their grandchildren before they all left. The children were older and more secure in themselves, ready to take on a new challenge with their parents.

Both Maya and Hannah were torn about leaving Grams and Grandpa Neil. "Everything is so unsettled right now. We can't ask them to move with us," Maya proclaimed.

"I know. They have a life in Maine and their own plans. But I want them to come." Hannah sighed. *It's so selfish of me. This is the biggest challenge I'm ever going to face. I need their strength and common sense.*

James hired a real estate firm to sell their house and Hannah's condo. Everyone was packing, trying to decide what to keep and what to sell. "Is it worth it to move the furniture to New Zealand?" Maya asked him.

"The way I look at it, if we buy our furniture there, we have the chance to meet local business owners and get a feel for the community in Queenstown. We can give Grams and Grandpa Neil some special pieces to hold for us if we want them later. What do you think?"

Maya sat on the nearest chair in their living room with her eyes opened wide. "You know, I just want you, the children, and our pictures. Furniture is just something you sit on."

James laughed at that. "We can sell the furniture as part of the house if the buyers want it. Whew! This is the start of a whole new life, isn't it?"

"It is, indeed," Maya agreed.

✦✦✦

Grams and Grandpa Neil were excited for them and decided to take Chelsea and Bobby out for ice cream sundaes before helping them to pack.

"Well, Bobby," Grandpa Neil said. "What do you think it will be like there?"

"Mom showed us all the pictures that she took. It's so different from Ohio! But where else would I meet other kids from China, Tanzania, or Guatemala? It's like parts of the whole world will be there with us. And it's an island—ocean all around. I'm gonna learn how to dive and look at coral reefs under the sea!" Bobby's voice rose as he told them about his new adventures.

Grams smiled and looked at Chelsea. "What about you, sweetie? Are you excited about going to New Zealand?"

Chelsea hesitated, twirling her braid around her fingers before responding. "I'm a little bit afraid. But as long as I have music, I think I will be happy." She sighed. "I'm going to miss you."

That was too much for Grams. She started to tear up and reached for Grandpa Neil's hand.

"It's not like you're moving to another planet. We'll keep in touch," Grandpa Neil said. "I want to hear about all your adventures, both of you. We'll use that conference call software, Zoom, or one of the others. And if you're really good, Grams will send you her special cookies."

Chelsea and Bobby both laughed and dug into their sundaes.

✦ ✦ ✦

For Hannah, the moving process was bittersweet. Like Maya, she wanted only a few things—her pictures, her bow and arrows, and a few special gifts made by children she had taught. *How I envy Olivia! She quit her job, packed in one day, and flew off to New Zealand to find a new place during the project construction.* Hannah felt like her entire life was being conducted via computer. She was losing her connection to people. Being with people was *necessary* to remain human. The experiences people had when they were together created meaning and caused people to grow and change. This enlightening thought was interrupted by the doorbell.

"Coming! Just a minute," Hannah called from the kitchen.

"It's just us," Grams said, opening the door. Grandpa Neil followed behind her.

Hannah met them in the living room. She wanted to remember this moment. Two of the people she loved most in the world were standing in front of her—Grams with her wistful smile, causing her dimple to appear, and Grandpa Neil, standing straight and tall, holding something behind his back.

Hannah hurried into Grams's arms to hug her tightly before they had to leave. The smell of orange blossoms would always remind her of Grams's shampoo. She inhaled deeply, then turned to Grandpa Neil.

"So, what's behind your back?" Hannah challenged.

"Oh, just a little something to remember us." He offered her a beautifully framed picture of the two of them, standing in front of their home in Maine. A glimpse of the garden could be seen near the bottom, and the trees were just starting to flame into color.

Hannah hiccupped. "Oh … my! This is wonderful. I never would have been able to do this without the two of you."

"You know, we're just a phone call away. The obstacles you've overcome so far are just preparing you for the harder ones to come," Grandpa Neil warned.

"I know you're right about that. But I have good people helping me. Who knows what tomorrow will bring? New Zealand is calling me, and I must go. The real work begins now." Hannah smiled, her grey-blue eyes bright with emotion.

Chapter 15: Adisa Buhle

In Tomas Ojeda's first assignment as a newly hired Accelerator, he was meeting children and their families in countries he had never visited before. Today, he was landing at the Mount Kilimanjaro Airport in the northwestern part of Tanzania. The early morning sunshine streamed in through the windows as the 747 touched down.

Tomas was there to see Adisa Buhle, a girl of nine who had caught the attention of teachers and religious and municipal leaders for her incredible insight into people and events surrounding them. Her file said that one day when she was seven years old, she walked across the schoolyard to speak with an older man there to meet his grandson. She asked him to accompany her to the nurse's office. When she entered, she told the nurse that the man was getting sick and needed help. The nurse saw that the man was having a little trouble breathing and listened to his chest with her stethoscope. The arrhythmia she heard was beyond disturbing. She called for an ambulance while Adisa held his hand and told him, "It will be okay now."

Tomas looked at her picture as he waited outside for a bus to take him to her village. The day was warming up, so he quickly moved to a bench shaded by a large fabric awning. He saw a sweet round face and twinkly brown eyes surrounded by long, curling black hair. Adisa's family lived in Arusha, just west of the area dominated by Mount Kilimanjaro. The

Arusha National Park contained lakes, grassland that sustained native animals such as giraffes, and old volcanoes. He wondered what it would be like to grow up in the shadow of the largest mountain in Africa.

How will I convince Adisa to leave her family and her country to join the project? Will her family see that she is needed to help a larger cause?

The bus took Tomas to the village where she lived. The homes were newer than he expected, arranged in neat rows with space for trees and flowers between them. Her entire family, including a black-and-white border collie, was there to greet him as he climbed down the bus stairs. Adisa, smiling in a cool summer dress with white sandals, stood quietly next to an older woman with streaks of gray in her braids. A tall Black man, dressed in a cotton tunic and pants, stepped forward with his hand outstretched.

"I am Julius Buhle, Adisa's father. Hannah told us that you are from Guatemala. Welcome to Tanzania! Can I help you with your bags?"

Tomas bowed politely and reached out to shake Julius' hand. It was wide and strong, with calluses along the ridges of his fingers. "Thank you for such a lovely greeting with your family. I am happy to be here. Tanzania is quite breathtaking. I only have one bag and can carry it easily. Would you please introduce me to everyone?"

Adisa stepped forward then and asked her father, "Can I do this, Papa? It will help him to get to know the family through my eyes." Julius smiled and nodded to her. Adisa took Tomas by the hand and looked into his eyes. She blinked two or three times, then she pulled him forward toward the woman with the braids.

"This is Nona, my mother's mother. She is the best baker in the village. She also plays the pipes. I have listened to her music every day of my life." Tomas bowed, taking her wrinkled hand in his. She pulled her hand away and gave him a gentle tap on the nose.

"Silly child! Don't treat me like a princess! Treat me like your *abuela!*" she admonished him.

What a surprise! Tomas chuckled and said, "S*i, Nona.* I'll come for treats later." Nona smiled at him and walked up the path to the house. Adisa took him to her mother next, one of the most beautiful women he had ever seen. But it was the compassion in her face that held him silent.

"How brave of you to come so far to meet our Adisa. Let's go inside for the rest of the introductions. It is getting hot, and I have made some *horchata* especially for you."

Just then the dog came over and sat on Tomas' feet. Tomas put his hand down so that the dog could smell him. When the dog began to wag his fluffy, black-and-white tail, Tomas scratched the ruff around his ears and whispered something to him. The dog stood, looked back at Tomas, and started toward the house.

"He's the final word on who comes in," Adisa said as she gave the dog's fur a ruffle and skipped up the path. The house was built like a large square, with the gardens and cooking ovens open in the middle. Each side of the house had its own function: To the north were the bedrooms and bathrooms.

The east side held work rooms with large windows looking out at the mountains. The south side faced the neighborhood, with entry areas for guests and a library. The west side rooms were the most surprising; art, photographs, musical instruments, tribal masks, and plants were everywhere.

Later that day, Tomas met Adisa's older brother and sister after they returned from school. They all chatted amiably about the happenings of the day, trying to make Tomas feel comfortable in the group. Dinner was a delight for the senses, with vegetables, barbecued meat, and several sauces that made each bite different. Nona brought out a braided loaf with fruit, glazed nuts, and powdered sugar for dessert.

This will be harder than I thought. Who would leave this loving family? There is so much joy here. I can only hope that Adisa's empathy will open her mind to our cause.

Tomas ate far more than was good for him, and he asked if Adisa would take him for a walk around the neighborhood. Julius approved on the condition that they take the dog with them. While the older children cleaned up, Julius said that he and his wife would review the day's receipts from their veterinary business.

The neighborhood was quiet after the dinner hour. The setting sun painted the sky with orange and burgundy flames against the deepening blue. Tomas noticed the air was subtly scented with herbs and flowers that smelled like lavender.

"Please, tell me about this special place for children like me," Adisa said during the walk.

"It's hard to describe the place because it is not physically there yet. Our founder, Hannah, has a dream about helping children with unique abilities work together to do things in new ways. We are all seeing the damage being done to the places where animals live with pollution, fires, and storms. The oceans are being filled with plastic and dangerous chemicals. Even the air is harder to breathe than it once was. People who make money by doing things that cause damage don't want to change. But if we don't change, we will destroy each other, the animals, and all that we love. When you look at the world today, what do you see?" Tomas asked, eager to hear Adisa's perspective.

"I hear people fighting because they don't know how to listen. I feel hunger and pain from many animals. I see light trying to fight the darkness, especially when families love each other. But there's more distance between us all now."

Adisa was quiet for several minutes as they walked in the warm evening breeze. Then she said, "What I feel from you is hope. I see patterns when I look at people or hear them or feel them. Sometimes, I can see what they will say or do next. When I talk with Mama and Papa, they say it is the way I use my senses. Maybe it's a smell coming from the person or the way their eyes move. Maybe it's a lot of things that I don't know how to explain. Mostly, I try to keep away from danger. That's how animals survive. But whatever this is, I can use it to help. A while ago, my brother was about to do something really stupid that might have ruined his life. But I could see it coming, so I asked him to stop. Thank goodness, he trusted me and listened. He has grown up a lot since then." Adisa became quiet as they turned back toward the house.

Tomas sighed as he realized it was time to ask the hard questions. "Would you leave your family, your home, and your country to become part of Hannah's dream if your parents supported it? That is the reason I came to Tanzania to meet you. There is a lot for you to think about, Adisa. You are still very young to be asked to make such big changes."

She stopped walking, calling the dog back to her. Tomas kneeled down to pet the dog and look into Adisa's face. She took a deep breath, nodding her head slowly. "Nona says I must understand why I have special gifts. It's more than helping our family. Maybe I need to meet other children with special gifts to understand. I'm not afraid, I'm just not sure."

"When I was growing up in Guatemala, my abuela told me the same thing. It is only now that I am finding my way," Tomas explained. "I decided to learn as much as I could. I went to school every day and then to college when I was older. I did learn many things, but not much about using my own gifts. Now, I think I am getting another chance to find out." Tomas felt that he had done the best he could to help Adisa make her decision.

"It is getting late, and Mama will worry if we are not back soon," Adisa said. "Thank you for coming to see us. I don't think I will sleep very much tonight."

Tomas took her hand as they walked up the hill, with the dog leading the way. *Adisa is unique. I wonder if I can convince Nona to come with her to New Zealand. That might make everyone feel more comfortable and provide Adisa with family to keep her grounded.* Tomas knew that Adisa was right. To work with her family, he needed to listen.

Tomas had three more months of travel for interviews before he would move into the temporary staff quarters in New Zealand. The Technology Institute had generously offered some rooms in the student dormitories for the Accelerators to use. He was anxious to see how the construction was going, and to experience New Zealand for himself.

Chapter 16: Hahona Manaaki

If Hahona Manaaki decided to join Hannah's project, he would be one of the younger students at the facility. A native Maori child, his parents were anxious for his heritage, his love of nature, and his healing skills to be a part of the human evolution project.

Hahona's skin was golden brown, and his muscles were already well-developed at age ten. His voice was soothing, with a hint of music behind it.

When Hannah met Hahona for the first time in New Zealand, she decided to take him to the location where they were building the Bridge to Forever. It would span one of the deepest gorges in the forest, connecting the east and west sides of the mountain range. Hannah wanted to know what Hahona saw when he looked at it.

To build that bridge, Hannah and Olivia had searched for a design-build team to create a bridge that incorporated aspects of the forest as well as modern components for strength and durability. The anchors on both sides were made of reinforced steel. The suspension structure was made of braided cable, with slimmer cables hanging down from the upper level to merge with thick wooden supports. Hannah especially loved the woven sides, which were made of fishing nets that had been used by the Maori people for centuries. The walkway was a textured sheath of thin metal that blended seamlessly with the other components. The braided wire suspension had been anchored to massive trees on either side of the gorge. The nets, walkway, and wooden supports were stacked in a clearing 100 meters back from the side of the gorge.

With a month of fair weather ahead, the bridge could be completed in five weeks, saving the project more than $100,000 in estimated labor costs. Then testing and inspection would finish this part of the project.

"I have been reading a lot about the Maori people," Hannah said. "But I don't suppose I can really understand what it means to you. Would you please tell me about yourself and your family?"

Hahona looked at her face. Hannah thought that he was probably very good at detecting the truth and lies by using his senses. He hummed a soft song and stood, listening to the echoes and the responses from the forest creatures, before he answered her.

"The Maori are explorers. Legends say we were sent by the gods to take care of the sea and the land. I am one of six children in my family. We all have certain things that we love. In Maori, my name means 'healer.' That's what I will be when I grow to be a man. Do you know many healers?" he asked.

Hannah thought back to her experience with Maya after the car accident. "When I was about your age, my sister was hurt very badly, and the doctors didn't think she would survive. I loved her very much and somehow, I knew that my love would help her. I think that healers are drawn to places, to people, and to things that need them. They're able to share and give what they have to make things better."

Hahona nodded. "Yes, that is right. It is not always doctors and pills. Sometimes it is music, or sunshine, a touch, or water—so many different things. The healer knows what is needed.

"Two years ago, I was training with our Elder to start healing. A woman named Jabiri was going to have a baby, but she started hurting inside. The Elder wrapped her in blankets and then told me to sing to her. I didn't know what to sing, so I chose a song my mother sang to me when I was a baby, which always made me feel safe and loved." Hahona paused, closing his eyes and breathing deeply. "Jabiri stopped crying. She put her hands against her middle and started to sing the song with me. The Elder told me that Jabiri would be okay, so I left."

Hannah saw the compassion shining in his face. "Did she have her baby?" she asked.

"She had a big boy with a head of curly hair. Jabiri named him 'Whirikoka,' which means 'strength' in Maori," Hahona explained. Then he reached for Hannah's hand and held it between his own. "You are afraid to fail. But I feel the burning inside you, the hope, that we will make a difference."

Hannah gasped and started to tremble. *How perceptive this child is. And all of this from just touching my hand. I wonder ...* Hannah looked across the gorge. "Here we are building a bridge. I brought you to this place so that you could look through your Maori eyes and tell me what you see."

Hahona looked around him and then down to the stream that flowed at the bottom of the gorge. "I see all the parts nearby. What I feel is the bridge will be built, but it is the wrong kind of connection. Nature created this space between the mountains with a purpose that we have not understood. There are other things that can replace the need for a bridge. I'm sorry, but I do not see more than that," he said.

Hannah thought about what he said. A child's perspective and respect for nature created a new pattern. Wasn't that why the project was being created? "Thank you, Hahona. How does your family feel about you joining us in this project?"

"My family wants to save our history and make a place for us in the world. I am the link to the future. I want to meet the other children and the teachers. I want my healing skill to grow."

"Yes," said Hannah. "I think we'll be helping each other. There is so much hurt that needs to be healed. We look forward to you joining us here."

Chapter 17: Sister Angelique and Father Brennan

Olivia followed up with the next important step to stabilize relations. "I have an idea that I want to run by you," she told the Finance Team . "We need to establish a regular channel of communication between our project and the surrounding communities. Maya, James, and their children went to the local church over the weekend, where they met Sister Angelique. Maya told me that she could be the link we need to start the local communications channel."

"I'd like to meet her," Hannah said. "You're right. Local communication is so important. Maya is the best choice for building good relationships with our neighbors. She is so down to earth. And the church will have more personal ties with the community than the institutions we have been working with for the past few months."

Later that day, Hannah and Maya went to the church to meet with Sister Angelique, who was all business. She was short and round, with rosy cheeks, dimples, and curly brown hair. "Welcome to our church!" Sister Angelique said as she pulled Hannah into a quick embrace. "I am so happy to meet you, Hannah. You are younger than I expected. I do love that twinkle in your eyes. I am very busy today, but Father Brennan wanted to meet you both and has offered to take you for a brief tour. How does that sound to you?"

Maya looked at Hannah, who smiled her approval. "Father Brennan is a very dynamic man," she told Hannah.

Sister Angelique said, "He was amazing during the COVID-19 pandemic. All communities were especially hard hit until the vaccine was available. We saw so much distance develop between families, friends, and businesses and even the church. Father Brennan went to the United States to obtain vaccinations for our church staff. That enabled us to reach out, ensuring that people felt cared for and important, that they were not alone. Here he comes."

Father Brennan's red hair was peppered with streaks of grey. Hannah thought that he was in his mid-forties and just over six feet tall. He looked like a man who never stopped moving, slim in a healthy, active way.

"Father, this is Maya Suweto. Her family came to services last Sunday," Sister Angelique said.

Father Brennan reached for her hand. "I remember you. I always look for new faces in our congregation. God presents us with so many opportunities to grow and learn."

"And this is Hannah Larsen. She is head of the project being built not far from here." Sister Angelique nudged Hannah forward.

Hannah was hesitant in the face of this human dynamo. But she wanted to make a good impression, so she reached for his hand, putting forth her best smile. "I am so pleased to meet both of you. What a lovely church you have, especially the wooden doors with the beveled glass cross insets. When lit from behind, they would be a bright invitation to come inside."

Father Brennan tilted his head to one side, gazing at Hannah with wide eyes. "So, you are a person who sees what can be, a dreamer. I am a seeker. I look for the good in people." He paused at a nod from Sister Angelique. "Time is running short, and we are keeping the good Sister from her work today. The SUV we use for traveling around the community is just over here."

Hannah and Maya had a hard time keeping up with Father Brennan's long strides. He invited them into the SUV and drove east to show them other churches in neighboring communities. He talked about the history of the South Island, how it was originally settled by three Maori tribes from the North Island and later influenced by Dutch, French, and English explorers. Even the Chinese came in the 1800s during the gold rush in the Otago region.

"How did all those different people and cultures influence the island's development?" Hannah asked.

Father Brennan took a moment to prepare his reply. "It feels like New Zealand received the best that each of those cultures had to give. We have fantastic music, art, and architecture. We have people who care deeply for the land and its plants and animals. There are savvy businesspeople, deeply religious communities, and so many people eager to learn. And the food! Wait till we get to Alexandra," he teased.

As promised, they stopped in Alexandra for lunch at a local bistro that was obviously a favorite stop for the locals. The noise of customers talking, ordering, and grabbing to-go lunches from the counter had Hannah's head in a whirl. Father Brennan brought them to a table outside and went back inside to order for them. Maya pulled out her water bottle and offered some to Hannah.

"Whew!" Maya said. "I hope Bobby and Chelsea can keep up with him because I sure can't!"

"Being with Father Brennan does feel like riding the tail of a tornado, doesn't it?" Hannah commented.

He walked out a few moments later with a large tray. Glasses of iced tea clinked merrily. A large shepherd's pie sat in the middle of the tray, with a short stack of bowls and silverware beside it.

"Lunch is served, ladies. Please dig in," Father Brennan said as he deposited the tray on the table, sat down between Hannah and Maya, and promptly began dishing out the pie for them.

"Yummm," Maya said after the first bite. "I've got to remember this place." She pulled out her phone and started taking pictures.

"Maya!" Hannah said, "I'm hungry, too, but shouldn't we say grace first, Father?"

Father Brennan started laughing. "God's grace is always on us when we are together. Do you think God would mind if we enjoyed the bounty of this Earth he has given us? I, for one, am always grateful, especially when new friends come into my life. I was blessed to feel God's presence when I was a small boy. We all struggle through hardships, joys, and sorrows, learning each and every day, and finding love in all of it. One of the most important lessons to learn, and to teach, is tolerance. God had a hard time with that one early on. He left it for us to find a way."

Who is this amazing man? He has just the attitude I was hoping to find. His support would go a long way. Father Brennan was right. Lunch was delicious. He actually seemed to slow down a little after the meal, so Hannah decided to question him about his knowledge of the project.

"Father Brennan, thank you so much for that lovely meal. I'd like to ask what you know about the project we are involved in. It's not a secret or anything, but the community might not understand what we are trying to accomplish."

"We couldn't help but notice the construction crews going in and out of the forested land. And frankly, Sister Angelique and I started researching your project on the internet soon afterward. It's always good to know something about your neighbors. We were hoping that you would come to us before we used our government contacts to find out more."

So they are resourceful, curious, and well-connected, Hannah thought. *He didn't really answer my question though. Pushing him could destroy the connection we are trying to make here.* Although the thought of revealing more about the project caused Hannah's hands to shake, she decided to trust him.

"Father, we are building a place where people can work together to find new ways to solve problems. We believe that the answers will come from the unique perspective of special children. That has been our challenge—to find children and young adults from all over the world with the potential to create real change." Hannah took a breath but held up her hand, signaling that she had more to say.

"The trouble is that the problems are getting much harder to fix before the damage becomes permanent. The methods being tried by countries now are too slow. We're hoping to find a faster way."

Father Brennan rested his elbows on the table, clasped his hands together, resting his chin on them, and closed his eyes.

Hannah looked questions at Maya, who only shook her head.

"Amen," Father Brennan said, opening his eyes to look at them. "I envy you this adventure. In truth, you will no doubt find many obstacles in your way. Just a warning, where the light shines brightest, there the darkness is drawn. Be watchful and careful."

Chapter 18: Tamlyn Reiter

Accelerator Amanda Collins read through the file on Tamlyn Reiter, age nineteen. Amanda had been assigned to meet with Tamlyn and her family in Vienna to see if she wanted to join the XL-ENCE project. Her biological adaptation was entirely unique: She could blend into the shadows, becoming undetectable to the human eye.

Tamlyn's application had been submitted by a biology professor at the University of Vienna named Andrei Bauer. A few days before her visit, Amanda called Professor Bauer to find out more about his work with Tamlyn.

Professor Bauer said that Tamlyn was showing more control of this ability as she grew older; however, it was not exactly available on demand. He stressed that because it was present in her genetic structure, she was certainly a good candidate for the XL-ENCE project.

Amanda wasn't sure if Tamlyn knew that he had sent in an application for her, and she wondered what would happen when they met.

"Mom, Amanda Collins is here," Tamlyn called out when the doorbell rang.

When the door opened, Amanda saw a healthy young woman, with light blonde hair, a thin face, and freckles.

"Please come in," Tamlyn said, leading her toward a cozy living room with an inviting fire merrily crackling in the fireplace.

"Hello, I'm Amanda Collins. Professor Bauer contacted our project, and well, he thought given your special abilities, you might be interested in working with us. Will your mum be joining us?"

"Um, yes. I think she's putting the dishes away," Tamlyn said. "Here she comes. Mom, this is Amanda Collins."

"Please sit down. Would you like something to drink? Coffee or tea?" her mother asked.

"Thanks so much. I'm fine. I really want to talk with you both. Tamlyn, will you tell me about yourself?"

"Well, I grew up here in Austria. My mom and dad liked to take me hiking in the woods when I was little. When I was old enough to go to school, I met other children; some were nice and others were bullies. I was afraid of the bullies because the biggest boy threatened to hit me if I didn't give him my lunch one day. I ran down the hallway and sat down behind a trash can. I tried not to cry or make any noises. Then he walked right by me. I saw him clearly, but he didn't see me." Tamlyn took a breath and continued. "My mom told me that she also had this ability to hide when someone threatened her and somehow become just another shadow on the wall. Later, when I became interested in biology in secondary school science classes, I studied Darwin's theories about species evolution."

Her mother explained more recent events. "Tamlyn earned a scholarship to the University in Vienna when her high school paper on abnormal genetic development in animals caught the attention of the head of the Biology Department. While Tamlyn is attending the University, she is studying her own blood, skin cells, and genomic structure. Professor Bauer is very excited about it."

"Well," Amanda began, "Professor Bauer sent in an application for Tamlyn to join us in the XL-ENCE project. Children from all over the world will join us in this study of human evolution to learn how to combine their unique skills to solve problems, especially those related to how humans interact with their environments. If you are hearing about this for the first time, I'm sure you have lots of questions. Feel free to ask them now, and I'll do my best to answer."

Tamlyn's mother started first. "Children from all over the world? Where is this project located?"

"We are building the facility in New Zealand. It's a beautiful place on the South Island."

"Why do you think I should join this project?" Tamlyn asked.

"Part of the project is to study whether the unique skills of the children involved can be genetically transmitted, as we can see with your mother and you, Tamlyn. We also want to strengthen and broaden these abilities by presenting Challenges that teams will work on together. Professor Bauer thought the study of human genetic development in Hannah's project was the next logical step for you."

Amanda left them to discuss the opportunity overnight. Tamlyn had so many questions and was hoping that joining the project in New Zealand would provide direction for the use and expansion of her knowledge and skills. She convinced her mother and father to let her try. She could always return to Austria if it didn't work out for her.

$$\maltese \ \maltese \ \maltese$$

A few weeks later, when Tamlyn arrived in New Zealand, her first meeting was with Hannah, whose new office was in the administration building on the northeast side of the complex, facing a waterfall tumbling gently down the mountains behind it.

Hannah said, "You're not a child or an adult yet. That makes it difficult to develop a program for you because you're older than the children here but younger than our Accelerators—the young adults who help to challenge and work with them. You are the first example of a genetically transmitted adaptation in modern people. I would like to assign you to work with Amanda on the Accelerator team for a while, as sort of an assistant Accelerator. How do you feel about that?"

"Frankly, I understand that I don't really fit in here, but this is an entirely new environment for learning. I have been wrapped up in my biology research for a long time. When Amanda told us about the environmental aspects, I kept thinking about Darwin's observations about animal adaptations for survival. I haven't paid much attention to climate change or water or air pollution. I guess it just feels like part of life." Tamlyn stopped talking, but she felt her face growing warm with embarrassment. "I guess that's a pretty selfish and irresponsible way to live. If I can observe the Accelerators working with the children, it might be helpful for me to see how they use their special skills. When I met Amanda in Vienna, she seemed like a nice person. She asked me a lot of questions, but I don't think I answered them very well."

Tamlyn had met other students at the University who were outstanding in their fields. Some were eager to learn and develop in their areas of interest. But others were naturally gifted. They seemed to understand how things worked at a deeper, instinctual level. *But how could those instincts apply to advanced areas like astronomy, technology, and architecture?* Tamlyn wondered

"Don't worry about that," Hannah assured her. "This is new for all of us. Please try working with Amanda for a while and see how it goes. But we're on a tight schedule at the moment. Probably the most critical part of this whole project is learning to work together. We'll all take language classes so that we can communicate with and show our respect to each other. That respect also extends to the land and the community around us. James Suweto and Lei Chen Xiao are supervising the Accelerator group. If Amanda is not available, you can also talk to them. Do you think you can be patient?" Hannah asked.

I can do this. I just need to use my observation skills. Think of it as being in another type of classroom. Tamlyn lifted her chin and nodded to Hannah.

"We are not a real team yet. I'm glad you and your family decided to work with us. And don't forget to reach out to the children. They have some amazing stories to share. Welcome to the project." Hannah stood, and then she swayed momentarily from side to side. "Whoa, that was weird! I got a little dizzy there for a second. I look forward to learning from your point of view. Please share your thoughts and feelings with Amanda. She is a good person." Hannah reached forward to shake Tamlyn's hand.

Tamlyn left Hannah's office and headed back to her room in the newly constructed staff quarters, a two-story building with wide windows to let the cool evening breezes in. She slowed down, walking carefully around the site and observing the people working and the beautiful trees and the waterfall in the mountain behind them. As she came upon a secluded meadow, she could feel herself beginning to absorb the smells and colors around her. She watched her skin as it began to change. A groundhog emerged from a small hole close to where she stood in the shade of the trees. It watched her for several minutes, then dove back into its hole.

The next day, Tamlyn asked Amanda if they could talk for a while between classes. Amanda suggested that they meet for a late lunch. "I'll bring food," Amanda said. They agreed to meet outside the cafeteria building currently under construction. Amanda carried two bags and a thermos in her hands. "I thought we could eat outside," Amanda said, holding up the lunch bags. "It is still warm, and we'll be away from all the noise in there," she said, nodding her head toward the classrooms.

Amanda led Tamlyn to the patio area outside of the nearby medical facilities building. Lunch was ham sandwiches, with chips, and the thermos was filled with tomato soup. They ate in comfortable silence for a while. Then Tamlyn started to fidget.

"What's on your mind, Tamlyn?" Amanda asked.

"I've been watching the other students and the Accelerators as they work together. I understand why they are part of this project and what their abilities can do to make the world a better place. But I don't see where my abilities fit in. What do you think I can contribute to mankind's development? My skills are mostly instinctive and for my own protection. How is that going to help other people?"

Amanda waited, trying to find the words that would acknowledge Tamlyn's feelings, without giving her false promises. "Those are good questions, Tamlyn. It sounds like right now, you feel like an 'odd duck.' Believe it or not, most of us experience a period in our development where we don't feel like we fit in either. I think that working through the Challenges together will help you see your way, even though I don't have any answers for you now. Most of the children here are learning how to use their unusual qualities. It might be that your skills must be joined with others' to be most effective."

Amanda watched Tamlyn's face fall, so she continued, "Mostly, we don't want you to be hard on yourself. Now is a time of learning. If you keep an open mind and heart, you'll find your place."

"I hope so," Tamlyn whispered.

Chapter 19: Hannah and Nicholai

Hannah could not drag herself out of bed. When the phone rang, she was not sure she had the strength to answer it. "Hello?" Hannah wearily asked.

"Hannah, sweetie? Is that you? You sound terrible! Or is it the connection?"

"Grams? Oh, Grams. I'm so glad you called. How are you and Grandpa?" Hannah asked between coughs.

"We are fine. But you clearly are not. Don't make me come out there. You are to stay in bed with tea and a warm blanket until you fall asleep. No arguments, young lady. How will your fabulous project succeed without you? I am going to make a few calls to make sure things are going well. You will not answer the phone, get on the computer, or even watch TV today. Do you understand me?" Grams sounded concerned but firm.

"Yes, Ma'am," Hannah said with a hitch in her voice. Their love had sustained her through many teenage traumas, the death of her father, love affairs gone wrong, and other missteps. "I love you, Grams. We'll talk again soon. Yes?"

"Of course, sweetie. Now, go to sleep. We love you."

It was quiet in Hannah's cottage. Sarah had found it for her shortly after the site purchase was settled. Hannah made herself some tea and crawled back into bed. Before the tea was finished, she found just enough energy to put the teacup on the night table. She burrowed under the covers and slept the sleep of the dead.

Hannah's dreams were scattered and fragile. Faces swam by her, blurring as they passed. She sat atop a mound of contracts that must be read and signed, but try as she might, the mound never seemed to get smaller. The most disturbing dreams were scenes of forests burning that blended into skyscrapers with slums buried in their shadows. Every time she tried to raise her head, she felt dizzy and went back to sleep.

Bright sunshine greeted Hannah as she opened her eyes and looked at the clock. It was 10:30 a.m. A knock at the door pulled her out of bed and into her bathrobe. Hannah slid into her slippers and walked carefully to the door. She was still wobbly but felt much better than she had when Grams had called. She looked through the glass in the front door to see Nicholai standing on the landing. She opened the door, then blushed, remembering she was still in her bathrobe.

"Hello, Hannah," Nicholai said. He had a vase full of colorful flowers, a bag, and a jug dangling from his left arm. "I come bearing gifts!" He led Hannah into the kitchen, placing the flowers on the table. He went to the cupboard and pulled out two bowls, some spoons, and plates. Hannah sat in a kitchen chair and felt the sun streaming through the window, warming her back.

"What's all this, Nicholai?"

"Hannah, you've been out for three days. Because you didn't reply to our emails, texts, or calls, someone came in and checked on you every day. Dr. Stanley took blood, checked your heart and lungs, then pronounced that you needed rest. He put bottles of water next to your bed, assuring us that you would drink them, whether or not you were fully awake. Your body knew what it needed: sleep and water. I don't think anyone even tried to wake you. You must have had some pretty weird dreams because all of us noticed you were mumbling and sweating at times."

"Three days!" Hannah stuttered to a stop. *No wonder I felt so crappy.* "What's going on with the project?"

"Later," Nicholai said. "Much later. I brought some soup and a loaf of Shepherds bread. I thought you might need some sustenance, and I wanted to talk with you. We haven't really talked since the expenditure review with Stephen several weeks ago."

The soup smelled wonderful, and Hannah's stomach started growling almost immediately. Nicholai smiled, poured them each a bowl of soup, and cut the bread, smeared it with butter he found in Hannah's fridge, and set it on a large plate between them on the table. Then he sat next to her and began to eat.

"I suggest you dig in before the soup gets cold. It's best when it's hot. And I fear that your stomach is demanding attention," he said.

They ate companionably until their first bowls of soup were gone. Then Nicholai refilled Hannah's bowl, made some tea for himself, and opened a few windows to let the sweet-smelling air flow through the room.

"How have you been, Nicholai? Where are you staying? And P. S. thanks so much for the soup. I really needed it." Hannah reminded herself to be thankful that so many people cared about her. She still had so many questions about the project's status.

"First of all, please start calling me Nick. Nicholai sounds so formal. At the very least, we are good friends, as well as partners on this project. Second, I have been busy getting to know our Accelerators and the children. I understand what you meant when you said that the project wouldn't really come into focus until the children were here. They are completely amazing! And Logan, Amanda, Tomas, M'gera, and Teani introduced themselves to me and Stephen. I just can't say enough about them."

Hannah couldn't stop tears from coming to her eyes as she watched Nick's face light up while he was talking. That's how she felt about the project and what it would mean for the world.

"Hannah, are you crying?" Nick asked as he wiped a few tears from her cheeks. "Maybe you should lie down on the couch for a while." He led her away from the table, sat her on the couch, and covered her with the knitted afghan lying across the back of it. Then he sat next to her and took her hand.

"Hannah, please talk to me. You being sick made all of us realize how much we need you to be with us. What is going on with you?"

"Nicholai, Nick … I never get sick! I feel so stupid. Everyone is working hard, and I spend three days in bed. What kind of leader does that?"

"No one, and I mean *no one,* can go through what you're doing without getting worn down. We're not robots, Hannah. Most of us are here because we feel compassion for others. How can we not feel that for you?" He stuck out his tongue and made a face at her.

Hannah laughed; he looked so funny. "But how can I thank them? Money seems so inadequate, so shallow. Why are they doing this?"

Nick saw the tears forming in her eyes again. He pulled her into his arms. "If Maya or Olivia were here, they would give you a big hug. Since they're not, the job falls to me. When I was recruited and you explained the project, I saw the intensely bright light that came from inside you. I looked around to see if anyone else could see it. Turns out it was just me. I can't explain what that light did to me. It pierced me, the dream, the vision. But it was also you. I believe that many things came together when you were given that money. You allowed yourself to open up. Maybe I can explain it better later. I'm not the only person who believes in your vision. We all have different reasons for being here. But this project is *important.* Every time I hear a newscast, read a newspaper, or listen to people complaining, I know that humans need to change. We need to evolve. We are all here for that purpose: to ensure the continuity of the human race and the Earth."

Hannah pushed away from Nick slightly so that she could look into his eyes. "That is your skill, putting everything together and seeing what's ahead. Thank you for coming here to tell me this." *I've spent so much energy trying to convince other people that we had to start NOW that I didn't realize we'd already begun.*

"How about a nice, hot shower?" Nicholai suggested. "I'll clean up our dishes and check on you when you're finished."

"That sounds like heaven. If you wait for me, could we go for a walk?" Hannah asked.

"Let's see how you feel. If you're not wobbly, we will walk, but just for a little while. You still need your rest."

"Be right out," Hannah smiled and disappeared into the bathroom. But after the shower, toweling her hair dry made her tired. She draped the towel over the shiny chrome bar and wandered toward the bed. *I'll just lie down for a minute,* she thought as she drifted into a deep, healing slumber.

It was two days later before Hannah was fully rested. She returned to work, determined to catch up. But, after a few days at her desk, she woke up feeling worn-out again. Hannah realized that something was needed to replenish her energy. She decided to invite Nick to join her for a picnic at the edge of the forest near the new outdoor barbecue grills and oven.

"Hi, Nick," Hannah said when he answered his cell phone. "How would you like to join me for lunch today?"

"Need time to clear your head?" he asked. "I sure do. Meet you at your office? Or shall I pick you up in the jeep I bought last week?"

"It would be great if you could pick me up. My head's still a little fuzzy. Hope you like turkey sandwiches. I've got some leftover pasta salad that we could have with them. Does that sound okay?"

"Perfect. I'll bring some fruit and water. See you in about an hour," Nick said.

A cool breeze greeted them when they arrived at the edge of the forest. Nick spread a blanket next to a fallen tree, where they could have their picnic in the shade. They chatted about how the project was going as the food was laid out, then they dug into the sandwiches like starving children.

"Where did you get this pasta salad?" Nick asked.

"Maya made it. We have a standing tradition of dinner together once a week, just the two of us. She always cooks. She likes to try new recipes out on me before she gives them to her family. Bobby and Chelsea will eat almost anything, but believe it or not, it's James who is the picky eater," Hannah explained.

They finished the meal and packed up the leftovers, sitting quietly under the trees. Hannah smelled the crisp scent of the pines. The bubbly stream made soft music in the background. *We're so lucky to have found this place.*

"Take a walk with me?" Hannah asked.

Nick reached for her hand to help her stand. "I have a long stride. Think you can keep up?"

he challenged. Hannah skipped ahead, and he quickly caught up with her. They found a path leading around the base of the hills, just perfect for taking in the beauty of the forest. Hannah felt her head clearing and her heart rate slowing. This is what she needed. The energy of the forest was gentle, soothing, and filling her with renewed strength. Nick started humming softly.

"What are you singing under your breath there?" Hannah smiled at him.

"It's a song my mother used to sing to me when I was young. I haven't thought of it in years. But being here made me remember how it made me feel. My parents have been gone for a while. They loved and cared for me all my life. I miss that."

Hannah stopped and looked into Nick's brown eyes. The flecks of gold were as stunning as she remembered. "I don't know what it is about you, Nick. I feel like I know you. The underneath you, where your heart is free. You are so intelligent and insightful. But the man who was singing a few minutes ago is someone I want to know better. You understand the flame that is in me. And I can see the light that's in you—it's your compassion."

Hannah saw Nick's eyes light up with joy as he squeezed her hand. "I would be honored. This is a task worthy of gods or saints. We're neither of those, but we are determined, caring people who just might be able to make it happen."

Chapter 20: Gustav's Parents

Gustav began packing up his office at the university on a warm Sunday morning in late June. The end of the school term had been hectic, but he had finished grading the final exams and posting the scores on Friday. He could continue with business transactions from his apartment. He had moved the chemical compounds from the lab to a storage unit before finals week. Shipping could continue from there until he moved to the new project site in New Zealand.

As Gustav pulled letters from the bottom drawer in his desk, he found one from twenty years ago. He fell into his office chair, once again experiencing the dramatic events that occurred when he was fourteen ...

That year, he began to notice that his mother was changing. She still tried to protect him from his father's violent temper, but the actions she took did not make sense to him. She would take him into a dark room at the side of their house and ask him to be very quiet. Then she would *change. She seemed to be disappearing before his very eyes.* As she walked toward the door, her skin took on the darker colors of the walls and textures of the furniture. When she looked back, all he could see was her eyes, staring at him from the darkness. He could hear his father raging when she opened the door. He listened for his mother to speak with his father, but she did not speak at all. Slowly, his father would calm down. When it became quiet, he knew it was safe to return to the study to finish his homework. A few minutes after he left the side room, he could hear and see his mother in the kitchen making dinner. He wondered if his sight was failing or if something else was happening. His mother stopped returning from his father's enraged rants with bleeding lips or bruises on her face. Sometimes, Gustav would find his father passed out on the couch, the smell of alcohol on every breath. He was hopeful that the fighting had stopped, but a few months later, his mother went out for a walk and never came back.

Gustav became more active in hiding himself from his father. He took odd jobs in the nearby village, saving the money to sustain him after he graduated from secondary school. He was most fascinated in his work for the pharmacist, Herr Josten. Combining chemicals in specific ways to cure diseases, to ease pain and suffering, to strengthen the body was fascinating. And the money! People never argued over the cost. They just paid. He asked Herr Josten to teach him about chemicals and how to use them.

Herr Josten laughed, "It will take four years to give you a basic education about this! I don't have time. I work at the pharmacy all day and sometimes at night for emergencies. When do I have time for myself or my family? If you want to learn this, go to university."

Gustav was always a good student, but now he needed to be the best to qualify for a scholarship. His father would never pay for him to get a higher education. And just before he graduated, he got a letter from his mother that was delivered to the pharmacy:

> *My dear Gustav,*
>
> *It has been hard to be away from you for so long, but I am very proud of you. I can see great things in your future, starting with the Institute for Technology in Karlsruhe.*
>
> *You should know that I am well and happy. I divorced your father and remarried a wonderful man. You also now have a half-sister who is four years old. I hope we can be reunited one day. It is still too soon for me to reveal where we are living. Your father is vengeful and quite capable of killing us all. But I will watch as you grow and contact you as I may. Take care of yourself.*
>
> *Your loving mother,*
> *Viktoria*

At eighteen years old, Gustav was stunned. His father would not talk to him about his mother after she disappeared. He had imagined that his father hunted her down and hurt her so badly that she didn't survive. He scanned the letter for traces of where it might have come from, but could not find any. Shafts of jealousy pierced through his stomach, causing him to double over. He gulped air to keep from blacking out, abruptly sliding down the pharmacy wall to sit on the floor. So, she had escaped and now had a happy family and life! She left him to fend for himself. And so he did.

He realized that he could not be distracted by this now. He was on his way! He was controlling his life! He would achieve great things. Someday, he would have the resources to track his mother down.

As Gustav packed, his mind turned back to his father. Gustav knew his father had died many years ago. After his mother disappeared, his father sold the house in the forest, then purchased a lavish apartment in the city. His penchant for controlling everything around him finally earned him some equally violent enemies. Years later, when Gustav was in college, it was discovered that his father had been systematically draining funds from the company's medical insurance plan, decreasing the amount of coverage for the employees' job-related injuries and illnesses. He imagined his father loudly protesting his innocence and threatening the investigators who found him out. Rather than referring the crime to the corporate attorneys or local police, employees of the company decided to "retire" him early. They never found his body.

Gustav was notified when the bank contacted him about the past-due mortgage payments on the apartment in town. He put it up for sale as quickly as he could and used the money to continue his experiments, submitting his graduate work for publication to make his name known.

Gustav had never heard from his mother again. The anger and jealousy bubbled up in him as though it was yesterday. It was time to find her. He might be able to track her down using the resources from the project he was joining. And his half-sister, he would need to find out about her.

She had grown up with everything he never had: a warm, loving home; no fear of saying the wrong thing and getting beaten for it; no need to hide if her father had a drink or two.

Gustav developed several ideas for how to execute his revenge. He knew that some drugs could be used to make people highly suggestible. Others could make them sick, slowly over time. He decided to dedicate the next few months to finding chemical formulas that he could synthesize from readily available compounds. If he had time, he could test them on animals with brains and body chemistries that were similar to humans'. He would be quite busy for the next few months. He knew that he would be closely watched when he started at the new job. He didn't want any interference with his plans once he started them in motion.

Chapter 21: Time to Celebrate

When construction of the last buildings on the flat meadowland was finally completed, Hannah suggested to the Management Team that a celebration barbecue was needed. Summer was just beginning, with the smell of chive blossoms in the air and bright green leaves shining in the hills. Olivia, Maya, and James volunteered to coordinate the celebration.

"Here's how I see it," Olivia started out their meeting in the Admin conference room. "We can assign tasks to each group of people—the Management Team, Accelerators, the children, the teachers, and the support staff. Or we can let the groups pick."

"That's not going to work," Maya said. "We will definitely have to assign a task for the children. We should all think of their safety first. They could prepare simple desserts and side dishes. What do you think, James? It will be like when we had Bobby and Chelsea start helping us with meals in our kitchen."

"I agree. We could prepare recipes for them to follow using simple tools and give them help with baking and the ice cream maker," James said.

"Okay. What's left? Cooking the main dishes, setting up and taking down the tables and chairs, and cleaning up. The Management Team should be in charge of ordering all the supplies. Stephen and I can handle that," Olivia said as she started making notes on her laptop.

"The Accelerators should definitely do the cooking," Maya pointed out. "The support staff should set up and take down the tables and chairs so that no one gets hurt. Then they can just enjoy eating with the rest of us."

"That leaves the teachers to do the cleanup. We should set up bins for recyclable materials and trash. Then they can head to the kitchen to wash the pots, pans, and serving dishes," James noted.

"Good. The weather is supposed to be great at the end of the week," Olivia said. "That gives us four days to prepare. Maya, could you prepare a flyer? I know you are very artistic because the recruitment ads you created were very inviting! Let's get the flyer out tonight. James, please check with the medical staff to see if any of the children have food allergies we should be aware of. Let me know right away. Stephen and I will probably place the order tomorrow morning."

"Will do," Maya and James said at the same time. They all started laughing and split up to work on their jobs for the barbecue.

✦ ✦ ✦

Gustav von Telleman, who had arrived at the campus a few days prior, was now the chemistry teacher for the project. He woke early on the day of the barbecue. *Let's see what's going on outside. This is my chance to observe the other teachers, the Accelerators, and the students,* he thought. This was his usual pattern, hiding his true nature from new associates. He looked for those who could be a potential ally or a threat. *There is not much time to explore before I will be tied to classes and meetings. Such is always the case in new jobs.*

Gustav had read the file of a native Maori boy in the student population. Gustav scanned the children working at a few of the tables, trying to see if he could find him. He spotted a boy preparing a salad of greens and herbs. Perhaps he would be able to tell him about native plants and where they grew.

"Oh my!" Gustav said, approaching the boy. "That looks delicious. I am Professor von Telleman. I will be teaching chemistry and perhaps other science classes. But for today at the barbecue, we will eat and get to know each other. What is in the salad you are making?"

Hahona turned away from the table and offered Gustav a slight bow. "It is nice to meet you, Professor. Sorry, my hands are dirty. My name is Hahona Manaaki. I found these leaves in the meadow not far from here. There are cresses and tender greens that grow in streams. I also put in some herbs: thyme and a little mint."

"I see. What are you using as a dressing?" Gustav asked.

"We use nut oils, citrus juice, salt, and seeds to make dressings for greens. You are welcome to have a taste and let me know what you think. Adjustments are easy to make with all the supplies we have."

Hahona placed a few spoonfuls onto a plate for him. Gustav gingerly took a bite of the salad, chewing it slowly to try to identify the different flavors.

"Is that fennel I am tasting?" he asked. "The salad is quite good. I believe that there are nettles in there as well."

"Yes! We are very careful about using nettles in New Zealand," Hahona said. "One of the varieties, taraonga, can cause paralysis. It is very dangerous and grows wild in many places. The animals won't go near it, so we can tell what plants to avoid. Excuse me, but I must get back to my dishes for the barbecue. I look forward to talking with you again." Hahona covered the salad with an elastic-banded cloth and headed with it toward the kitchen.

When Hahona entered, he saw Adisa Buhle working with Enrique de la Vega, a new child from Brazil who had arrived at the project about a week before. They were making passionfruit-flavored ice cream for dessert. They had just finished heating the cream, eggs, and sugar mixture when Adisa felt her stomach clench, which was a sure sign of trouble.

"Is something wrong with the cream mixture, Adisa?" Enrique asked, as his blue-green eyes searched her face.

"No, the ice cream is okay," Adisa responded. "We just need to blend the passionfruit with the cream mixture, and then put it into the ice cream maker." Her stomach continued to bother her as they finished making the ice cream and put it into containers to store in the freezer.

"You are still upset about something. I can see it in your face," Enrique said. "Do you feel sick?"

"You are kind, Enrique. I'm not sick, but I don't know how to explain what I am feeling. It feels like being afraid. But I'm not afraid of you or anyone else I have met here."

"Maybe you should talk to someone about it? How about Logan?" Enrique suggested the red-haired Accelerator from Ireland.

"I think I'll look for Tomas. We've talked about things like this before, and I think he'll understand," Adisa said. She folded her apron and put it in the kitchen laundry bag, then hurried out of the swinging doors. *Where is Tomas?* she wondered, as she ran into Logan almost directly outside of the kitchen entrance.

"Good day, Logan. Do you know where Tomas is? I really need to talk to him." *Could Logan help me? I don't really know him.*

"Adisa, you're shaking! Did something scare you? I'm sorry, but I don't know where Tomas is right now. Will you let me try to help? What is bothering you?"

"I ... don't know how to explain it. I just have a feeling that something is wrong. I can't pinpoint the location. Right now, it is just feelings, and I don't know what to do about them." Adisa grasped her hands to keep them from shaking.

"I believe you, Adisa," Logan assured her. "If we walk around, do you think that will help?"

Adisa shook her head. That was one of the most troubling things to her. There was no one place that the feeling was coming from. "That's why I wanted to talk with Tomas. He has experience with feelings like this. Do you know what I mean?" she asked Logan.

"We all have natural intuition about danger, and we can often sense when something is wrong. I don't know what I can do to help you right now. If your feelings get stronger, find one of the Accelerators right away. I will tell Tomas and Hannah what you said. We will be on the lookout for trouble."

Adisa nodded, but she did not think they would be able to find the problem. *He doesn't sound like he believes me. I know this feeling.* Her stomach was still knotted as she walked back to her room in the student dormitory. Just before Adisa reached the door to her building, she saw Tomas approaching.

"Adisa, wait!" Tomas called. She waited until he was closer.

"Logan told me you were feeling upset and afraid. Can you tell me what's going on?"

Adisa related her physical reaction while she was preparing dessert in the kitchen.

"You've had this reaction before when there was trouble?" Tomas asked. Adisa nodded. "Why not give your grandmother a call? She might be able to help you."

Yes, I need to talk to Nona, Adisa thought. Adisa waved goodbye, then went into her quiet, peaceful room.

Adisa's grandmother came with her to New Zealand to ease the family's fears. Adisa was quite young, but she wanted to do what she could to help. Nona moved to Queensland, and she instructed Adisa to call on her cell phone whenever Adisa needed her. She went to her room, placing a quick call to her grandmother.

"Nona, I need to talk to you," Adisa's voice was shaking.

"I hear fear in your voice, little one. What has happened today?"

"We're having a barbecue for everyone at the project. I was making some ice cream with a boy named Enrique when my stomach started to hurt. I didn't feel sick. I felt that something was wrong."

"That has happened before. You should always trust what you feel. Close your eyes and describe the feeling to me."

Adisa sat in a lotus position on the floor and closed her eyes. This was a meditative pose that her mother taught her when she was very young. It helped to calm the mind and center the spirit.

"I felt a dark shadow," Adisa described. "It was cold. It moved around outside when I was in the kitchen. My stomach was cramping, and I bent over. Enrique asked if I was alright. I didn't know what to say to him. He saw the fear in my face. The shadow started to fade, but the feeling didn't go away."

"Poor child. Did you talk to Tomas?" Nona asked, remembering the young man who helped her move with Adisa to New Zealand.

"I couldn't find him at first, but I saw him and will talk to him again later."

"Good. If the feeling gets worse, I will come and stay with you. Be careful. Call me tomorrow, okay?"

"Yes, Nona. I'll be careful."

✦ ✦ ✦

Hannah was really pleased with the success of the barbecue—until Logan tracked her down in her office at the end of the festivities. "Adisa told me she was feeling upset and afraid, so I sent Tomas to talk with her," he said.

Hannah pulled out her phone and called Tomas right away. "Hi, Tomas. Logan says that Adisa was afraid of something, and you went to talk with her. What did she say?"

"Adisa felt that something was wrong near the project. I'm sorry that I missed the opportunity to be with her when the feelings occurred. I might have been able to help her describe the danger she felt. She called her grandmother, who is staying in Queensland and will be visiting the project a few times a week."

Where do we go now? She is so young, but her perceptual ability is the reason she is here. "Tomas, what do you think we should do? I want to believe her, but ... " Hannah hesitated to say more.

"I *do* believe her, and I think the staff should all look for places, people, and animals that could pose a danger to us here. I think I'll call Nona myself to see what Adisa said to her. Adisa is still scheduled for classes. I think it will be good for her to be with the other children. I'd like to invite Nona to come visit."

"That's a good idea. I'm sure Adisa will be happy to see her. Please keep me informed. And tell her that we will all be especially careful and watchful."

As Hannah sat at her desk, rubbing her forehead and wondering what to do next, she noticed a letter in the middle of her blotter that hadn't been there earlier that day. *One letter. No other mail. Who put it there?* When she opened it, she was shocked at what she saw.

Dear Hannah,

Every person who accepts a challenge must be prepared to face Disaster because whether you have a plan or not, disaster will find you. There is always the chance that, if you don't face it, you will be defeated. But take heart. Once you perceive the danger, you can take action to neutralize it. Use your resources. Just take the first step, and then the next.

Remember, you have already overcome many obstacles. Disaster just has a more sinister name.

Your friend and benefactor

Hannah called Nick, asking him to meet her in her office as soon as he could.

"Thank you for coming so quickly," Hannah said. "Have you met Adisa Buhle? She is from Tanzania and has amazing perceptual abilities."

Nick nodded as he sat in one of the chairs opposite her desk. "Go on. Something has gotten under your skin. What is it?"

"Adisa felt something dangerous during the barbecue. Some of the Accelerators worked with her to see if she could identify something specific. They believe that her perception is accurate. Have I been so wrapped up in making this project come to life that I neglected to assess possible dangers? What do you think we should do?" *If we screw this up, the money will be gone for sure. And just when we are getting started. What a nightmare!*

Nick walked over to the cut glass bottle of brandy kept in a nook of the bookcase. He poured the golden liquid into one of the glasses.

Hannah stood and walked over to him. "Here," Nick said, handing her the glass. "Drink this. And no arguments."

Hannah sipped the fragrant brandy, relishing the sweet, oaky flavor as it slid down her throat. *What a day!* "Nick, don't try to protect me from this. We need to figure out what to do next."

"For Adisa, danger could mean a great many things," Nick said. "Tomas is the best link we have with her. Let's compile information from Tomas as he works with Adisa. As she works to strengthen her abilities, she may be able to tell us more. Then we can look for a pattern. How does that sound?"

Hannah nodded. "I wonder if the danger is just developing. Maybe that's why she couldn't pinpoint what it was or where it was coming from. We need someone to explore the forest around the site. You've met our newest Accelerator, M'gera Kumalo, right? She's from South Africa, with a deep connection to the natural environment, and so she is the best person for this. She'll be able to sense if something unnatural is happening there from the animals and birds."

"Hannah, we have a lot of people here to help us. Communication and observation are our best tools now. Sharing information is the best way to move forward. Don't let the possibility of danger keep us from doing that."

Hannah was silent, holding her unfinished drink, staring out her office window into the darkness. "I'm scared, Nick. But that's what this project is all about: using special talents and helping each other to solve problems. I just wasn't expecting it so soon."

Chapter 22: Gustav's Secret

As Gustav searched for like-minded teachers and other adults working alongside him, he reluctantly determined that there were no potential allies to be found there. His comfortable one-bedroom apartment in the staff quarters was not private enough. His colleagues came by at all hours, all too often trying to engage him in chitchat and other unnecessary pleasantries. Gustav realized that he needed a place away from the project site to keep his private communications and experiments hidden.

Foremost in Gustav's mind was finding his mother who abandoned him when he was only fourteen years old. Gustav's mother kept herself and his half-sister, born after she remarried, well-hidden as protection from his abusive father. Gustav had spent many unsuccessful hours searching for them both before and after his father's death.

Now Gustav was living in a place where he was surrounded by exceptional children with supportive and caring staff. The contrast to his own childhood made the fire for revenge burn even hotter inside him. He had never had support like that. His brilliant, incisive mind would never be applauded by a loving family. It wasn't fair.

Gustav briefly investigated an apartment closer to Queenstown. But he considered daily commuting between the apartment and school buildings to be wasted time. He needed to find another option.

Worse yet, the Chief Operating Officer, Olivia Hutchins, wanted to meet with Gustav regarding how he was setting up his classes to teach chemistry to the children. *I'm regretting the choice to accept this position more every day. The salary is substantial enough, but I certainly had more freedom at the university. Now I must convince her to do things my way. My chemistry classes have been successful for college and graduate students. Simple revisions should work here.* Gustav headed to the Administration building. He remembered speaking to Olivia by phone before he was hired, but they hadn't met in person. Gustav anticipated meeting an elderly woman with grey hair and spectacles.

Olivia was certainly not what Gustav expected. Upon entering her modern, sparsely furnished office, he saw a woman in her late twenties or early thirties of medium height with light brown hair, a strong upper body, bright smile, and freckles across her cheeks. Olivia extended her right hand to Gustav as she opened the door to let him in.

"Welcome, Professor von Telleman. It's nice to finally meet you. I was hoping to talk with you at the barbecue, but I guess we missed each other," she stated, motioning him toward a comfortable-looking portable office chair.

"Yes, I spent a lot of time walking around the project site that day trying to get my bearings," Gustav replied.

"Unfortunately, I have back-to-back meetings scheduled for today. We need to discuss the methods you are going to use to teach chemistry here. For the past two weeks, most of the teaching staff has been talking with the children, either alone or in small groups, to prepare supply lists and content outlines. However, we don't have anything from you. Why don't you tell me what you are planning to teach?"

Having Googled her before their meeting, Gustav knew that Olivia's academic standards were high and that she would be expecting insightful teaching strategies from him. "I will submit a list of chemicals that are needed for advanced studies. Some of them are volatile and might take longer to be shipped here. I was planning to begin with basic experiments with easy to obtain materials and using the electron microscopes to look at chemical structures," he said.

"That's not going to cut it here," Olivia challenged. "Basic chemical experiments don't fit our project goals of achieving a better environmental balance between mankind and nature. I read that you are an avid climber and spend time in forest and mountain areas. Maybe you can work with our Maori student, Hahona, to learn about the chemicals being extracted from native plants."

It's good that I talked with that tribal boy at the barbecue. She won't be expecting this from me. Maybe I can put her off for a little while.

"I had a very nice conversation with Hahona during the barbecue," Gustav said, nodding. "He told me about the native plants he was using to make the salad. I was offered a taste and was surprised at how good it was. Unfortunately, we both had other things to do, so we parted quite quickly."

Gustav saw Olivia's eyebrows come together, suspicion evident in her glance. "You haven't really answered my question. How are you going to teach these children about chemistry that affects the environment?" Olivia asked.

She isn't going to let up on this. I had better do some planning as quickly as possible. Thank Gott the internet is available. And I will have some time to explore other areas as well, with or without the boy.

"This will take some thought and research. Is there a deadline for submitting my supply list and techniques?"

"Some classes have started, but more teachers will be joining us during the next two weeks. That will be your deadline. This information is posted on the website for all staff. Any supplies that need to be shipped in won't be available by that time. So, you'll need to work with what's available locally." Olivia stood and walked to the office door. "I look forward to seeing what you come up with."

Damn bitch! Gustav thought, but he smiled at her graciously and left holding his head up. *I can handle her. She's going to be very busy, and I don't have any students yet.*

When Gustav started researching the native plants, he remembered that Hahona had mentioned taraonga, a native nettle with paralytic properties. He could work with the students by comparing the chemical structures of the edible nettles and the taraonga plant. And he could start distilling the plant essence to test the strength and efficacy on small animals. He envisioned giving a cup of tea to his mother with the toxin and watching her slowly fall down a steep staircase, breaking her neck at the bottom.

As Gustav continued to use Google, he also found that the *Te Uru Rākau*, the New Zealand Forestry Service, had built facilities in many of the protected lands to preserve existing forests, promote regrowth of dwindling tree populations, and assist with fire prevention. During the COVID-19 pandemic, services had been cut back, and more surveillance was being done with drones and technology equipment at larger stations. *It is likely that there are unused cabins in the woods here. Perfect! I need ground maps. The construction crew should have updated maps right here.*

The next day as equipment was being unloaded in the eastern quadrant of the grounds for the gym, Gustav approached the construction crew foreman, Mateo. "Good morning! I am Professor von Telleman. You and your crew are doing a wonderful job. I'm very impressed at the way you incorporate native materials into the construction of our buildings."

Mateo nodded and motioned for the crew to keep unloading the pallet. "Hello, Professor von Telleman. Thank you for your praise. We are proud of our work, but we are very busy trying to finish by the deadline. What can I do for you?"

"I was wondering if you have any maps of the forest with paths and roads surrounding our facility that I might copy. I love to climb but want to avoid any areas that might be dangerous."

"Please follow me to my truck," Mateo said as he strode away at a brisk pace. Gustav hurried to catch up with him. Mateo said, "I have a map you can copy, and the bridge construction crew probably has a better one that you can use." He handed Gustav a map showing the construction area, roads in and out, and the building footprints in the leveled flatland area.

I really need a better map than this. It doesn't cover enough of the forest and mountain area. "Is it possible to talk to someone in charge of the bridge construction?" Gustav asked.

"I'll call the foreman on the radio to see where he is. If he's on his way down, I'll ask him to bring the map," Mateo said. "I've got to get back to work. Just put the map back in the truck bed when you're finished with it."

"Thank you so much for helping me," Gustav said as he shook Mateo's hand, noting the hard calluses and strong grip.

That afternoon, Gustav made copies of both maps. His inclination for secrecy kept him from talking in greater detail with any of the bridge crew. If anyone asked, it was logical for him to ask for maps to identify dangerous areas so that he could climb for exercise without getting hurt.

Next, Gustav planned for a three-day excursion to explore two to five miles in the northeast and northwest sections of the forest. He always moved with his camping and hiking supplies: large pack, canteens, walking sticks, pitons, fire and first aid kits, one-man tent and sleep sac, and dried food packets and cooking utensils. Any structures in those areas would be easy to reach from the construction area. He quickly posted his plant chemical comparison study to the project website, hoisted his pack, and left soon after dark to begin his search.

Chapter 23: Challenges in Queenstown

Olivia was impressed to see the Accelerators work together to develop Challenge tests for the children. Her oversight duties as the COO included evaluating this new technique to expand the children's special skills that were so needed to offset the more destructive traits of humans.

The tests were devised for teams. The children would work together, using their unusual talents to solve a puzzle, fix something that was broken, find something that was lost, or create something completely new. Challenges would be issued throughout the year to help develop their unique skills. Many of the Challenges would take place in the forest and nearby lakes. Some Challenges would be held in the neighboring community, which would give their neighbors a chance to get to know the children.

No child could fail a Challenge test because the object was to see how much their skills could be honed, expanded, and deepened.

Because Sister Angelique and Sarah Dowie continued to act as community liaisons, they participated in the Challenges to be conducted in community locations. Sister Angelique and Sarah knew that three children, including Maya's daughter Chelsea, were being given Challenges in Queenstown and Dunedin.

Suzanna Scott, an elegant Black woman, famed jazz composer, and performer from

America, eagerly accepted the offer to work with child prodigies. She taught Chelsea to develop her musical abilities, including reading music. Even though Chelsea was one of the younger children involved in the project, she was beginning to develop confidence, but she needed encouragement to interact with new people. Father Brennan invited the family to join the choir at the local church. Maya and Chelsea came to their rehearsals to learn the songs and harmonies. When playing the flute, Chelsea listened for the balance between the organ, the flute, and the voices. Members of the congregation told Maya and Sister Angelique that when Chelsea played with the choir, it was like hearing angels sing.

For Chelsea's Challenge, the Accelerators wanted her to play the flute with other musicians. Sarah found students in the Music Department at the University of Otago in Dunedin who were interested in playing with Chelsea. Chelsea's Challenge was to create an original piece for the quartet of flute, piano, bass, and conga drums, with a Latin flair, a new musical genre for the group to experience. Chelsea would perform the flute portion of the composition.

David Kamatsu, an American Accelerator with vitally needed computer technology skills, and fellow Accelerator M'gera were chosen to accompany the children for the Challenges conducted in Queenstown. During a meeting in one of the beautiful conference rooms, Olivia asked them for ideas for Karen Jeffries's Challenge. M'gera thought she had an answer.

"What is the best way to incorporate natural athletic ability into a new way to build the world?" M'gera asked.

Olivia cocked her head and smiled at M'gera. "Hmmm ... I picture those men who work on steel beams hundreds of feet in the air. They have to have good balance, extreme focus, and trust in their fellow workers. What kind of team would help with that kind of challenge?"

"Gymnastics comes to mind. They have balance and focus, but also grace and teamwork. What if we asked the Wakatipu High School girls' gymnastics team to work with us to build a rope bridge? And then to do a performance? Karen needs to learn the dance discipline the coach and team members can teach her. Karen can teach them about anticipating the way movement affects working together on the bridge. It is a new way to use Karen's skills and a different way for the team to see the future."

M'gera was talking to herself, but Olivia felt her excitement growing. "That's a good idea. Now your challenge will be to get your Accelerator supervisor Lei Chen Xiao to convince the coach and school principal to agree and to decide where to build the rope bridge."

"I'd love to do it here in the mountains, but they probably want to keep the students at the school. Karen will be comfortable there, so somewhere on the school grounds. A place where the other students can watch the performance and the bridge can remain up or be taken down," M'gera noted.

"If Lei Chen can persuade them, I'm sure they'll find a place. It was interesting listening to the way you thought about building a Challenge for Karen. I'm learning to look at the world through other people's eyes. And, in the end, I think it's going to be a great place to live." Olivia waved goodbye to M'gera, opening her laptop to post the Challenge for the Management Team's review.

That left building a Challenge for the young scientist, Emilio Ricci, the science wiz kid from Italy. David Kamatsu searched Emilio's file for information to develop a Challenge for him. He saw that he had been recruited by Teani, so he went to the staff quarters to look for her. Emilio was taking high school level earth science classes at twelve years of age before joining the project, and David wanted to hear what Teani learned about him.

"Emilio was just getting his feet under him when we met," Teani said after David tracked her down in the medical lab. "He lacked confidence, but he was eager to learn everything he could. I saw a pattern: He would listen intently, take information in, and then think about it. He would go through what he learned and then formulate his questions. Sometimes the questions would clarify his understanding; other times they would leap ahead. The sciences are his passion. He is interested in everything," Teani summarized as she walked with David outside.

"I watched him in class the other day," David told her. "Frankly, I don't think I can keep up with him." David blushed at this confession. He closed his almond-shaped eyes and shook his head, running hands through his dark, short hair. "If your description is accurate, my learning patterns are slower and require more interaction. How can I develop a Challenge for him?"

"Perhaps you can think of this as an opportunity to learn *with* him. You can share your observations and ask him what he finds. Our project purchased a new telescope for the Southern Technology Institute in Queenstown. How do you think Emilio could use it and work with the students and staff at the college to learn about the environment?" Teani asked.

"Maybe we could look at weather patterns. Earth's weather patterns are so difficult to study right now. But because the telescope might not be as useful as satellite information, I wonder if both instruments could be used," David suggested.

"If our goal is to come up with answers, we must first understand the questions. Emilio is great at asking questions. I think this would be a good place for him to start. The staff and students at the Institute will help him as well. Remember, no one can fail a Challenge. Even if Emilio does not understand weather patterns, he might discover something else that is just as interesting and valuable for our survival," Teani said.

"Thank you, Teani. I think I understand. I need to find out what the students at the Institute are working on. This is a Challenge for me, too."

✦ ✦ ✦

Later that week, on the ride into Dunedin for her Challenge performance, Chelsea sat in the backseat of the van with Bobby, quietly humming to herself.

"Is that from the composition you created for the Challenge exercise, Chelsea?" Maya asked from the driver's seat. Chelsea nodded. "Would you play it for us now?"

Chelsea was all smiles, realizing that her mother always encouraged her, even when Chelsea could sense she was worrying about something. She pulled her flute case up from the floor of the car, took out her flute, put it together, and began to play the piece for her family.

The music touched them all in different ways. Bobby clapped his hands in counterpoint to the rhythm. James sang bass notes to complement the melody. Maya loved hearing her whole family join Chelsea in her creation. She couldn't stop the tears from springing to her eyes. It was a magical moment she would never forget. And the full performance was just a short hour away.

After Maya parked the van, the family entered the concert hall, and Maya joined Sarah, Sister Angelique, and Father Brennan to stand against the back wall, watching the quartet as they played. Chelsea looked so small, sitting with the older musicians. But her face was shining with joy, as it always did when music was in the air. The Latin beat was so invigorating that the audience was soon on their feet dancing. Maya watched as Father Brennan spun Sister Angelique around and mamboed with her down the right side aisle. Sarah's blue eyes were wide as she applauded after the performers stood for their bows.

"That was amazing!" Sarah said to Maya. "And Chelsea wrote that piece? You must be so proud of her."

"I'm proud of everyone involved in this project," Maya said. "Chelsea has always been special to us. But now she has the support to make music into something that might help save the world. Imagine if the music she creates can calm people who want to attack each other or help to relieve depression or despair. Music can reach some people better than words."

Maya walked happily to the stage to congratulate the performers. Turning back to see if Sarah was following, she saw her standing in shock at the back of the hall. *Perhaps, instead of being just a liaison, Sarah is starting to see how important this project really is.*

✦ ✦ ✦

A few days later, Karen and M'gera watched videos in the gymnasium of balance beam routines as the most applicable form to relate to the bridge construction Challenge. At the high school, the gymnasts and the coach told Karen that the balance beam was the most difficult apparatus to master.

"Why is it so difficult?" Karen asked.

"The best way for you to learn is to get up there and walk around," the coach replied.

The gymnasts put large pads underneath the balance beam to cushion her if she fell off. However, Karen had no problem walking across the beam. After a few passes, she skipped lightly across and jumped off the end.

"How does she do that?" the coach asked M'gera.

"Karen has the ability to adjust to situations very quickly. My perception of this skill is that she can see what's about to happen and makes changes to her movements in a way that looks completely natural," M'gera explained.

"Let's try some somersaults to see what happens," the team captain suggested.

After just a few tries, Karen could flip, jump, twist, and somersault on the floor. On the balance beam, she fell off twice before she mastered the somersaults and flips.

"The dance parts are going to be hard for me," Karen told the team captain, which prompted the girls on the team to laugh.

"What's so funny?" Karen asked.

"Dancing is easy once you hear the music. A lot of your skills come from sports activities where there is no music. When you listen to the music, just let your body react to the beat, the instruments, and the flow. We'll show you."

One of the gymnasts walked over to a table against the wall and said, "Alexa, play *Roar* by Katy Perry."

Karen watched as each girl danced to a different part of the music. They all expressed themselves differently. One jumped into the air, splitting her legs apart and soaring like a bird flying. Another twirled around on one foot, going across the floor as if a magnet were pulling her and rotating her body at the same time. Her arms waved gracefully as she turned. The shortest girl clapped her hands, wiggled her hips, and made dramatic faces as the music pulsed and thrummed.

Wow! I need to find my own movements for the music, Karen thought.

"We practice our dance moves in front of a mirror that runs the length of an entire wall in another part of this building," the team captain explained. "Once we have mastered the dance movements, we incorporate the acrobatic elements to form a whole routine."

After that, it was Karen's turn to teach them about anticipating movement when they were working together on a moving surface. The trampoline was perfect for that. Karen started with two girls stationed one on each of the short sides of the trampoline. She told the girls to walk toward each other and then pass each other without falling. The closer they got to the middle, the harder it was to maintain their balance and keep walking.

"Walk faster, and when you get toward the middle, slide past each other, feet first, and then start walking again when you get closer to the edge and slow down," Karen said.

This worked perfectly, and by the end of the day, all the gymnasts were able to perform this routine smoothly.

M'gera brought the plans for the rope bridge to the school principal, who gave them to the school's shop classes. When M'gera explained what the performance by the gymnastics team and

Karen would be like, the classes couldn't wait to get the bridge built. They installed it outside above the campus grassy area, anchoring the sides to support poles framing the walkways. When the student body was assembled, martial music rang out as the gymnasts marched in and climbed to the ends of the rope bridge. They began their routine as the music changed to Katy Perry's *Roar.*

The girls danced out onto the bridge. The choreography was similar on both ends, but as they got closer together, the bridge swayed up and down, as well as back and forth. Then every other girl was tossed upward as her trailing athlete slid under her. The athlete in the air completed a back flip and, upon landing, slid under the girl above her in the air. The crowd had gathered, and they gasped as the flying, flipping, sliding girls never collided but successfully crossed over to the other side of the bridge by the end of the song. Wild applause rang out as they completed their routine. The team fell into each other's arms, laughing and pumping their fists in the air.

"Please stand with me under the bridge, M'gera and Karen," the school principal requested, then he announced to the assembled group: "I'd like to thank our neighbors, Karen Jeffries and M'gera Kumalo, for working with our gymnastics team on this special performance. And our thanks to the school shop class students, who built this wonderful bridge."

Whoops and laughter rang out from the students.

"Can I address the crowd?" Karen asked, looking over at the principal. He handed her the microphone and stepped away to stand beside M'gera.

"M'gera and I are part of a project to help people learn to work together to solve problems," Karen began. "I learned so much from the girls on the gymnastics team and their coach. I hope that I was able to show them a new way to use their amazing skills. I look forward to coming back and seeing you all again."

As M'gera drove Karen back to their new home, M'gera asked, "What are you thinking about?"

"I have a lot to learn," Karen replied. "I'm also concerned that connecting through athletics is not going to make the kind of changes that are needed for people and the environment to survive."

"Don't be too sure about that," M'gera said. "What if the school grounds were suddenly flooded and the students had to use the rope bridge to get to safety? Do you think they would be inspired by the performance today? That they would feel more confident that they could do it? I think they would."

Karen's face lit up. *She's right! Small steps first! Then we can tackle the bigger problems.*

"But more importantly, the community there feels positive about us, about XL-ENCE being next door," M'gera continued. "They will see us as helpers—not as a threat. That's also part of what the Challenges are built to accomplish."

Karen smiled and said, "I'll keep that in mind."

Chapter 24: Clues to Identify the Danger

Every night, Adisa and Enrique met with Accelerators Tomas, Amanda, and M'gera. Enrique provided information from the animals in the forest, especially the birds. They were disturbed by unusual activity northwest of the project site, so M'gera started her search in that region. It was a very large area, and she needed to be careful to watch the animals to see if they were detecting any danger. Caution made the search slower than M'gera would have liked, but it wouldn't help if she were injured through carelessness.

Adisa's sense of danger was growing stronger, but she still could not point to its source. Tomas and Amanda had other ideas for her that took advantage of her talents.

"Adisa, we think that you should start watching people who are moving around during the day. For example, we don't know much about the construction crew or the housekeeping staff. See what kinds of feelings you get when you observe them. Your feelings will help us to direct our attention where it needs to go," Tomas told her.

"Tamlyn might also be able to help us," Amanda said.

"She seems very interested in us. Sometimes, she sits quietly in the background in our classes. How do you think she can help?" Adisa asked.

Enrique responded first. "Her ability to blend in does not fool the animals. They know she is there. But she is not a threat, where this other thing is."

"Tamlyn's protective instinct should also be triggered when danger is near," Amanda added. "If the danger is coming from an animal, she might be able to hide for a little while, at least long enough to see what it is."

"I will ask Olivia to excuse you from your classes for the next few days, Adisa," Tomas said. "Remember, you need to start focusing on people who are here, including the teachers, administrators, medical staff, and even us."

The group broke up. The Accelerators went to Lei Chen to report in and then to Olivia. Adisa and Enrique returned to their dorm rooms. As they walked through the crisp night air underneath a blanket of twinkling stars, it was hard to believe that there was danger on such a beautiful, peaceful night.

$$\star\ \star\ \star$$

The next morning, Hannah went to town to meet with Sister Angelique and Sarah at the church to see if they could provide other information regarding danger to the project.

Sarah was the first to offer a theory. "Since 2020, there has been an influx of illegal drugs in New Zealand. Some are brought in, but others are being manufactured here. That's why access to the land you purchased for XL-ENCE was previously restricted and closely monitored. As you opened your facilites, the construction, publicity, recruitment, and the money have drawn attention to the possibility of exploitation. We cannot rule that out. I will talk to my law enforcement contacts to see what the criminal element is doing near Queenstown."

Hannah had been focused on the environmental problems, and she was surprised that Sarah thought that the project might be affected by other criminal activities. *This could ruin everything! What if criminals attempt to kidnap some of these extraordinary children and ransom them? How can we protect them from that? Truth be told, I would probably pay the ransom without hesitation to get them back.*

Sister Angelique furrowed her brow and said, "I don't see how the church can help you at this point. If Adisa and Enrique would like to talk or even come stay with us, we would welcome them at the church. They might feel safer there for a while."

"Thank you," Hannah said. "I'm anxious to see what you can find out, Sarah. We have resources at XL-ENCE that may help us find the problem faster. We'll keep you in the loop. Please contact me, Olivia, or Stephen if you find evidence of danger."

✦✦✦

The next day, as Adisa watched the construction workers during their final cleanup, her eyes kept coming back to one of the more skilled workers, who kept looking up into a particular spot in the forest. He worked hard during the day, and he occasionally looked around at the teachers and

Accelerators. As Adisa focused on him, her feelings told her that he was expecting someone to come ask him for assistance with something unrelated to the construction work.

Adisa left the construction zone to look for M'gera to tell her about the spot that the construction worker kept looking at during the day. Relief washed over Adisa when M'gera agreed to follow her to the site. *They do believe me! I wonder what M'gera is feeling when she goes into the forest.*

"When I was watching the construction crew today, one of the workers kept looking at a particular spot in the forest," Adisa said as she pointed to the area about 200 feet northwest of the project site. "What was it like when you were walking in the forest today?"

"I was much higher up than where you were pointing just now," M'gera replied. "I heard birds and small animals in the bushes. The wind carried the smells of growing things and water from the streams. It was peaceful. The land felt young to me compared to the mountains in Africa." M'gera bent down to look into Adisa's eyes. "Hmmm. I haven't checked that area yet. I was starting near the bridge and looking out over the streams. I'll start lower down tomorrow morning and have a look."

"Be careful. It feels to me like there is something there. It is not dangerous right now, but something is happening there," Adisa warned her.

"Thank you. I'll let Hannah and Nicholai know where I am going. I think that Tamlyn might be joining me if she has hiking and climbing experience. We'll be careful. Don't worry about that."

✦ ✦ ✦

That night, on one of his monthly visits, Stephen met with Olivia to go over the recent supply orders from the teaching staff. The big-ticket items, including a telescope, centrifuge, and electron microscopes, were on order and delivery was expected at the Technology Institute within the week. The smaller items were available locally, and Stephen would coordinate pickup of the supplies with the Accelerators or other staff going to Queenstown or Alexandra.

"Olivia, did you see the wacky list from Professor von Telleman on the website? Have you seen his lesson plans? Why would the Professor need lysergic acid, peptides, ergometrine, and cortisol? Isn't cortisol naturally occurring in the body as a result of stress? I would think a biology teacher would be more interested in some of these substances," Stephen said.

Olivia studied the complete list on the site. "Most of these chemicals are not harmful in themselves, but when they are combined, they can produce some pretty nasty substances." *Reminds me of when Mom and Dad were experimenting with mushrooms and peyote.* "Lysergic acid is the main component in the drug LSD, which produces hallucination, disorientation, and suggestibility. It's not a substance we really need or even want here for our students." *What the hell! I should have trusted my instincts when I reviewed his application letter.* "Please, don't order anything for him yet. I'll pressure him to revise his lesson plans and chemicals needed for them. Also, Hannah and Nicholai should know about this request."

"Thanks, Olivia. Per our instructions from Hannah, we look at everything twice, and if something feels wrong, it goes to the Management Team for review."

"We don't know what's wrong here yet, and this could be part of it," Olivia said. "We all need to be more aware of our surroundings. If Gustav asks you about the chemicals' delivery dates, tell him that supply chain delays and port inspections are affecting shipments. And that we don't know when we will be getting our orders."

"There are a few other unusual supply requests on the website, but nothing that seems dangerous," Stephen said. "Talk with you later at the next meeting."

Hannah, Nicholai, Lei Chen, Maya, and James quickly joined Stephen and Olivia for their evening Zoom discussion. After Olivia learned about the chemical supply order, she started thinking about weapons. "Before we started living on our land, our luggage was thoroughly searched. No drugs were found. Only some necessary medications were brought in. I brought my bow and arrows, not for defense or offense of course, but for relaxation. In New Zealand, guns are strongly controlled. I doubt that one could be brought in, and they would have been much harder to buy here after we arrived."

The group was quiet for a minute. James thought about what Adisa had been feeling at the barbecue and decided to speak up. "I think that Adisa's wrongness feeling would have been much stronger if there was a weapon on the project site. The danger would be more immediate."

"Has anyone talked to the Accelerators today?" Maya asked. "It's starting to feel like we all have little pieces of what's happening, but need someone who can put it all together."

"Tomas sounds like the right person for that," Nick said.

"You have that ability, too, Nick," Hannah said. "Why don't the two of you get together and start arranging the pieces?"

Olivia felt the frustration building inside her. The actions she could take to stave off this problem were so limited! *I need to get those revised lesson plans from the Professor. Then we will have some evidence of what he's up to.*

✧✧✧

Early the next morning, M'gera was ready to explore the region indicated by Adisa. Olivia told her that Professor von Telleman had gone camping in the forest, supposedly to look for plants to use for his classroom lessons. M'gera hoped to find evidence while she was checking the area today. She kept her binoculars loose at her side, and her maps, compass, and radio were carefully secured in her vest pockets. Rope, pulleys, and other climbing gear were stored in her backpack. M'gera was completing the final check of her gear when she heard a knock at the door.

"Can I come in and talk with you?" Tamlyn asked after M'gera opened the door.

"I've been assigned to scout the northwest area of the forest today," M'gera said.

"That's what I want to talk about with you. I'd like to help," Tamlyn said, blushed, and took a deep breath. "I am trying to find a way to fit in, to help if I can. Would you let me scout the area within five miles of the project grounds in that northwest quadrant? The animals in that area are not dangerous, plus I can blend into the darker parts of the natural background, so I won't be seen." Her eyes pleaded with M'gera for acceptance. "I can let you know if I find anything."

M'gera thought about it. Amanda had suggested that Tamlyn could be helpful as another set of eyes. They could keep in contact with radios and track each other. And M'gera already had another backpack filled with essentials sitting next to her desk.

"Have you done forest scouting before this?" M'gera asked. *Can I handle the responsibility of looking out for her? It would be terrible if she got hurt.*

"Yes. When I was young in Austria, my mother and father would take me for overnight trips to our local mountains. We often hiked all day. I haven't done much since I started college though. I'm in pretty good shape, and I can handle a short hiking trip today."

"Here," M'gera said as she handed her the backpack. "Try this on and see if it is too heavy for you. Lei Chen will need to give permission for you to go with me."

While Tamlyn tried on the backpack, took it back off, then rearranged some items so that she was more comfortable, M'gera called Lei Chen. He granted permission for Tamlyn to go, but he told M'gera that she was responsible for making sure Tamlyn was safe during the scouting mission.

"I understand," M'gera told him. "Tamlyn has experience hiking and climbing. We have radios, and she will stay closer to the flatland area. We should be finished before lunch."

M'gera filled a second canteen with water, handed it to Tamlyn, and together they walked out the back door of the building where they would not be seen by the work crews or other people at the site.

It didn't take long for M'gera and Tamlyn to reach the first section of larger trees. There they would split up, with Tamlyn taking the marked paths or following the smaller streams and M'gera climbing quickly toward the upper slopes. She selected a tall tree to scale for a wider view. *Same as yesterday—calm feelings around her, normal sounds, and usual smells.* M'gera pulled out her binoculars for a closer look, hoping that Tamlyn would be more successful.

✦✦✦

Tamlyn had been scouting for about sixty minutes when she came upon a clearing with an abandoned cabin in it. She circled the area, looking for anyone around the cabin. Then she peeked in the windows.

Who owns this cabin on the project land? Why was it built way out here in the forest? It looks like it had been abandoned for a long time. She could see boxes inside, so she thought that someone was using it. She shivered, and even though she desperately wanted to investigate the cabin, she knew that she needed to tell M'gera what she found.

M'gera had also spotted the clearing from her treetop perch, but when she tried to scan deeper, smaller trees and bushes around the clearing blocked her view. The radio call from Tamlyn brought her down the tree in record time. "Stay where you are," M'gera said. "Which side of the clearing are you in?"

"I'm on the southeast side," Tamlyn told her. "There is a large boulder next to the stream. You probably won't see me because I'm in the shadows, but I'll be near there. The boulder should provide some cover for you if anyone else comes around. The cabin looks like it's been empty for a couple of years, but I can see new boxes through the window."

"It won't take me long to get there. What else is happening?" M'gera asked.

"There are small animals and birds looking for food and nesting material. When I walked around the cabin, I saw a generator on the west side and a stack of wood. It looks like someone was testing the plumbing because there is water on the ground outside," Tamlyn said. "I don't think I should get any closer. Whoever is using this cabin might come back to check on it."

"I agree. Stay hidden and wait for me. Keep silent, no more radio communication. I'll be there soon," M'gera told her.

Chapter 25: Gustav Plans His Revenge

Gustav had hired a worker from the construction crew named Benito to move some of his class supplies and his generator to the abandoned Forestry Department cabin he had found about five miles from the facility on the northwest side of the mountain. The cabin was almost ready for him to start his personal experiments. *Now I just need to receive those chemicals I put on my supply list,* he thought.

The next day, Stephen told him that shipments had been delayed. Gustav figured that since Olivia had demanded that he focus on the environmental aspects of chemistry, he would have to start with the native nettle plants. *Maybe I can incorporate them into my own projects as well as the course curriculum.*

Gustav knew that money conquered most obstacles. If the shipment issues continued, he would use his own funds to procure the supplies. But then, he would need someone outside of XL-ENCE to place the orders for him and receive the shipments to keep his position clean. *I'll probably have to go to Queenstown to find someone qualified to help. The local pubs will be the best place to start.*

Because Gustav had been so focused on his own needs over his new teaching job, he knew he was behind in learning about his students and the

Accelerators, so he spent a few nights reviewing their files. The students had some unique abilities, but he didn't see a way to use them at this point. After several hours, he found an unusual file. This person, Tamlyn Reiter, was not a student nor an Accelerator. She looked oddly familiar in the pictures from her file.

Gustav couldn't believe what he was reading! Tamlyn Reiter was from his part of the world, with Austria bordering his homeland of Germany. She had the ability to change her skin tone like a chameleon. Gustav suddenly felt sick—sharp pains radiated from his stomach into his back and legs. He leapt to his feet and flung his chair away from the table, sending it crashing into the wall.

Was it possible that Tamlyn was his half-sister? Gustav was reminded of his mother's strange abilities that he had noticed shortly before she disappeared from his life. His mother seemed to fade into the shadows to hide from his psychopathic father.

Could she really be here? So much work to find them, and now my half-sister is here under my feet!

Gustav wondered if he could prove this assumption. Could he determine if Tamlyn really was his half-sister? He didn't have access to the medical laboratory. DNA testing would confirm the relationship, but he would need a sample to submit for testing. A simple cut from a broken beaker in his classroom would suffice to collect her blood. *How long would it take to get the results back? Too slow. A casual conversation with her might produce the information I need. And then if I'm right about Mother—a threat to Tamlyn might draw her to me here.*

Gustav was panting with anticipation of the revenge he had craved for so long. His heart was racing, scattering his thoughts like buzzing bees. *Calm down, dummkopf.* Gustav thought of the black void that was his preferred state of being. As the blackness claimed him, he retrieved the chair and returned to his desk.

In the meantime, Gustav would develop a plan. The paralyzing drug from the native plant Hahona had described presented a tantalizing possibility. If he could paralyze his half-sister, she would experience the pain he went through as a child, helpless at the hands of merciless adults. XL-ENCE staff would notify her mother, and she would come for Tamlyn. Oh! The pain she would feel!

There were many options, but he knew it would be best to make it look like an accident. He couldn't risk anyone knowing about their familial relationship. He needed to set off a tragic chain of events. He pictured Tamlyn dangling from the Bridge to Forever ... and falling, falling, falling into the deep canyon below.

✦ ✦ ✦

Two days later when Adisa entered the science building, the sense of danger she had been feeling for more than a month sharpened dramatically at that moment. She was astonished and afraid. Heading toward the language lab, she saw her friend Hahona talking with an older man in the hallway outside a classroom. *Who is that?* Waves of darkness seemed to emanate from him. *Poor Hahona! I've got to get him away from that terrible man!*

As Adisa walked toward them, the conversation stopped. The man squinted his eyes and raised his eyebrows.

Hahona made the introductions. "Adisa, this is Professor von Telleman, my chemistry teacher," Hahona said. "Professor, this is Adisa Buhle. She's a student from Tanzania."

"Pleased to meet you, Professor," Adisa said. Then turning to Hahona, she added, "I'm sorry to interrupt, but Logan has asked for you."

"Would you please excuse me, Professor? I should go now," Hahona said.

Gustav nodded his permission and turned back into his classroom.

Adisa grabbed Hahona's hand and quickly led him away. Once away from the Professor's classroom, she explained the urgency. "Hahona, I'm so sorry. I had to lie. Logan didn't ask for you, but I needed an excuse to get you away from that man. He's a very dangerous person." Adisa then described the fearful feelings she had been having during the past few weeks.

When Adisa started shaking, Hahona grasped her hand tighter. "I believe you, Adisa. He was asking me where to find taraonga, a paralytic nettle that grows wild on the South Island. Do you think he might hurt an animal—or even a person—with it?"

Adisa could only nod her head. "Yes. Let's get out of here. I need to tell Tomas about the Professor. And you can tell him about what he is looking for."

They found Tomas outside near the picnic tables. After Tomas heard what Adisa and Hahona had to say, he asked them to come to the Admin building so that he could set up a teleconference with Nick, Hannah, and M'gera.

"Hello, everyone," Tomas said. "Adisa and Hahona brought me updated information on the danger we are investigating." He quickly summarized the information from Adisa and Hahona.

"Adisa, why do you think the Professor would ask Hahona about that poisonous plant?" Hannah asked.

"I don't know exactly why he would ask about the plant, but I can sense that he wants it very badly," Adisa said. "I also feel that it would be dangerous for him to get it because it is the first step of many that he is planning."

M'gera gently cleared her throat to get the group's attention. "Tamlyn found a cabin about a third of the way up the mountain from the flatland. From the outside, it looks like it's been abandoned for a few years. Benito, one of the members of the construction crew, has been leaving work early and going into that area. We checked it out but didn't want to stay there in case he came back. Tamlyn spotted some boxes stacked inside the cabin and a solar generator and stack of wood outside in a sunny area near the back door. Because that cabin is on our property, the Forestry Service would have notified us if they were going to be using it again. Someone is preparing to use it. But why?"

"I'm going to get Tamlyn," Nick said. "We need her information to form a complete picture and to determine what the next steps should be. I'll be right back."

While waiting for Tamlyn to arrive, Adisa began taking deep breaths to calm down. *The danger is so close! What else can I do?*

Tomas watched her and Hahona closely as they talked with the adults. He sat next to Adisa and put his arm around her, whispering, "You are not alone in this, Adisa. Now that we know about Professor von Telleman, we can work together to find out what he's up to and then make a plan to stop him."

Adisa was not reassured because she sensed there was too much that could go wrong. When she tried to picture the future, she only caught glimpses of the mountain, the bridge, and the faces of Tomas and Tamlyn. She heard voices, but she couldn't tell who they were or understand what they were saying.

Nick returned with Tamlyn and continued the conversation. "We know the Professor is up to something, and we know that someone here used Benito to begin working in that cabin." Nick turned to Tamlyn and asked, "If we keep the Professor busy, do you think that you can get into the cabin and look around? With your camouflage ability, I think you're the only person who can safely make the attempt. What do you think?"

"I will do everything I can to help," Tamlyn said. "We need more information, and it's there in the cabin. I might be scared, but it is worth a try."

"I think we will have to act soon—today or tomorrow," Tomas said.

"It is supposed to rain in two days," Nick said. "That would be the best time for Tamlyn to check the cabin. It will be darker with more places for her to hide."

"I'll go with her as a lookout," M'gera said. "I'm not averse to getting wet, and I have all the gear we need to do this."

"Tomas, thank you for bringing this to our attention," Hannah said. "Nick and I will come up with a distraction to keep the Professor busy here. Good luck, everyone."

Before they ended the conference call, M'gera asked Tamlyn, "Can you come to my room now? We need an alternate plan for unexpected 'visitors.' It's always good to have other options. I don't want either of us to encounter them. Get in and get out—that's our main objective. If we don't find anything useful, we can go back another time."

Tamlyn nodded. "I agree. My main worry is that I might not *recognize* anything useful, even if I see it."

"Tamlyn," M'gera looked deeply into her eyes. "You must trust yourself. Use those incredible senses you have. And keep in touch with me. If you have a question about something you find, take a picture of it. We can talk about it later."

"Okay. Let's get ready," Tamlyn said, then she walked out of the Administration building toward the staff dormitory.

+ + +

Gustav was running some preliminary tests in his classrom on taraonga he had collected. He tasted a very small piece to note the effects. The taste was slightly astringent, and his tongue became numb for a little under an hour. He did not notice any change to his thought processes or the way his body felt. *Now to distill a liquid that can be more concentrated.* He was not going to test that on himself, but he thought he could add it to a sweet beverage to mask the flavor and serve it to Benito. They were almost finished moving the supplies into the cabin; tomorrow Gustav would pay him and celebrate with a drink.

The next day in the cabin with Gustav, Benito collected his pay and quickly polished off his drink. When he began to pack up his tools, he started to get so dizzy that he grabbed onto Gustav to keep from falling.

Gustav lowered him into a nearby chair and said, "Relax!"

"Oh no!" Benito said. "I feel very sick. I think I'm going to throw up."

Gustav grabbed a wastebasket and stuck it under Benito's head. Benito heaved up everything in his stomach for fifteen minutes. Then he started sweating, and Gustav laid him out on the floor. He observed Benito closely for signs of paralysis. Benito tried to talk, but his words were slurred.

Near midnight, Benito fell asleep. His breathing was normal, and he had no other signs of physical distress. Gustav realized that a more concentrated batch of the taraonga distillate was needed to give his half-sister the treatment he planned. *I don't have much time left. Better to make another batch now, even if I have to stay up all night.*

Chapter 26: The Benefactor

Later that evening, Hannah was on the phone with Nick. "Is there anything else we can do to figure out what's putting us in danger? How can you be so calm about this?" Hannah asked, then she started to cry.

Just then, Maya and James came over to her cottage, letting themselves in with the spare key Hannah had given them. Maya immediately went to Hannah, took the phone from her, and sat her down at the kitchen table.

"Hello, Nick," Maya said into Hannah's cell phone. "Just give me the quick-and-dirty update. I'll stay with Hannah. Go." Maya listened as Nick explained. She took a handkerchief from her purse and gave it to Hannah. "Okay. I think I understand. Let me go over it with Hannah, and I'll call you back later." She hung up the phone, pulled another chair over, and sat down next to Hannah.

Hannah stopped crying, turned to Maya, and said, "The worst part about this whole situation is that we can't reach out to our partners for help. I wish that local law enforcement could take over for a while. But we lack evidence. And we don't want them to think we're helpless. My gut tells me to protect the children and slow the project down."

James said, "Hannah, you're obviously feeling overwhelmed right now, with good reason. The stress of getting the project going; handling the money; managing teams, staff, teachers,

Accelerators; taking care of local communication and the children; and now dealing with the threat of danger—it's all happening so fast. Remember that we have resources here that law enforcement doesn't. Would they have believed Adisa? Or Hahona? You're right; they would dismiss our fears because we don't have hard evidence to support them. They've been trained to react *after* something happens. We're different, and we will find a way to neutralize the threat *before* it is unleashed."

Hannah looked at Maya and James. Maybe it was their experience with children, maybe it was their own special talents, but they never forgot the big picture. Thank goodness they decided to join the project; they were the ones she needed to keep her from panicking. But that didn't help her feelings of inadequacy, fear, and confusion.

Meanwhile, Maya was going through the pile of mail that had accumulated in a basket on the table. "Hannah, there must be three weeks of mail here! Look, there's an envelope from the estate lawyers. I am going to make us some tea. You should open that one first. It might be important."

Maya selected mint tea for herself and James, filled the kettle, and set it on a back burner. Hannah asked for rose hips tea. She started sorting through the mail, depositing advertisements in the trash can and local newspapers beside the reading lamp. The scent of tea steeping in the kitchen calmed her and helped her to refocus. As she sipped the hot tea, she reached for the envelope from the lawyers. Inside was a letter from her benefactor, with the missing information she had been waiting for.

Dear Hannah,

You may not remember me, but your confidence in our ability to achieve great things set me on the path to my many successes. One day in class, we talked about our hopes and dreams. I told you about my idea for an invention to reduce suffering, but I didn't think I could do it. You told me, "Why not? Albert Einstein wasn't special at our age. He just saw things in new ways. He allowed himself to follow his passion."

You inspired me to keep working toward my goal. In a way, you helped me to become the person I was meant to be. That is why I am giving you this chance to do something great. I know you will find a path that is uniquely yours. I have confidence in you. Here's hoping you will be the source of inspiration for others as you were for me.

Your friend,
Robert Langer

Robert Langer!?! Hannah remembered him from a class in secondary school. His words were surprising, and they brought up memories from long ago.

In the envelope, the lawyers had included magazine clippings from the period after his medical invention reached worldwide distribution. The first summary article read:

Robert Langer graduated from Massachusetts Institute of Technology with degrees in engineering and biology. In 1995, he discovered that a blast of low-frequency ultrasound could liquefy the mortar-like fat molecules in the skin, opening temporary gaps to allow large molecules to pass into or out of the body painlessly. This procedure was first used to extract animal venom or other poisons from the bloodstream. Later, it was used by people with diabetes to absorb the insulin needed to regulate their blood sugar levels.

The next article included more information:

SonoPrep, invented by bioengineer Robert Langer, is a device that delivers medication by sound waves rather than injection. According to the Sontra Medical Corporation, SonoPrep's manufacturer, the small, battery-powered device applies low-frequency ultrasonic energy to the skin for fifteen seconds. The ultrasound temporarily rearranges lipids in the skin, opening channels that allow fluids to be delivered or extracted. After about twenty-four hours, the skin returns to normal. His invention revolutionized medical treatment, and it was enthusiastically adopted by doctors, nurses, parents, and researchers.

Further information on Robert Langer included his contributions to the development of artificial intelligence as applied to robotic forms, other inventions, and his interest in environmental stability during the past twenty years. He participated in the development of lead-free motor vehicle fuels that significantly improved the air quality in California and New York. His more recent endeavors focused on corporate accountability for dumping pollutants into natural waterways.

Hannah was stunned. She silently handed the letter to James. "It's from our benefactor. His name is Robert Langer. I remember him from school." Hannah closed her eyes, picturing his eager, boyish face, short brown hair, shiny blue eyes, and shy smile. *He keeps sending hope my way. Thank you, Robert. I've got good people with me. We'll figure out how to defeat this monster, no matter how scared I am.*

She opened her eyes to see the surprise on the faces of Maya and James. "He says that I inspired him and that he trusts me to carry on with the good work he started," Hannah said, and then she smiled. "He faced his fears and worked through them. If he can do it, so can I."

✦ ✦ ✦

The next morning at 8 a.m., Tamlyn and M'gera headed out into the forest in the pouring rain. The project site was deserted. Everyone was inside either studying or attending classes.

"It's so quiet," M'gera whispered.

Tamlyn nodded in response. She began to absorb the feelings around her; the animals and birds were slowly going about their daily tasks. They seemed to be enjoying the fall shower. The woods provided protection for them. *I wonder where I can hide if someone shows up at the cabin.* When the pair got within fifty feet of the cabin and could see it clearly, Tamlyn motioned to M'gera to stop.

"I'll go on from here alone," Tamlyn said. "Don't forget to call to check in with me. I think your voice makes me feel safer." Her hands were shaking slightly.

M'gera noticed and reached for them to comfort her. "I'll check on you in thirty minutes. We probably have at least an hour before anyone shows up. Once you're in there, look for private correspondence, journals, receipts, and personal items like letters and photos. Don't take anything. Whoever it is would be very careful about the things he or she kept here. If you find anything you don't understand, take a photo on your phone. We'll figure out what it is later."

Tamlyn nodded and crept around to the back of the cabin. She was surprised to find no lock on the door and entered quietly. She saw that long tables had been set up with Bunsen burners, test tubes, a small microscope, and glass slides. *This must be a combination office and laboratory.* She didn't see any papers or research materials sitting out.

If I'm going to find the documents that M'gera said would help, I need to search in other rooms. An interior door led to an abbreviated version of a kitchen. It was obvious that the person didn't spend much time cooking or eating there, so she headed through the kitchen to the room at the front of the cabin.

Tamlyn saw a couple of chairs with a side table and lamp between them and a desk against the wall. On the desk was a pile of receipts, some order forms, and a checklist. The receipts showed that electrical supplies, distilled water, flashlights, and plastic containers were purchased within the past week. The checklist was even more interesting. *Look! Beakers, forceps, solvents, test tubes, and spray cans of compressed air. Laboratory supplies,* Tamlyn thought. *Why keep that list here? Sounds like it is for a class?* Because Tamlyn didn't understand why the list was in the cabin, she took a picture of it.

She looked around the living room for anything else that might be an indication of danger. Hanging on the wall, she saw a picture of a young boy, around fifteen years old. He looked very stoic, dressed in a dark gray suit and tie and standing in front of a school. It might have been a graduation photo. *Is that Professor von Telleman?* Tamlyn could read the words in the background: Waldschule Degerloch, in East Germany.

There's not enough here to determine intent. His personal items must be in the bedroom. She noted that M'gera's call was due in five minutes. She hurried into the next room to see what else she could find. The room was dark, and Tamlyn didn't see any lights or lamps. The window was small, and the louvered shades were closed to ensure privacy. She opened them to let in more light. Now she could see it was a bedroom with serviceable furniture of fairly good quality. She opened the dresser drawers to see casual clothing, sweaters, gloves, and knitted caps.

Where else to look? The door to the closet in the corner stood open. Tamlyn saw a backpack on the floor and glimpsed a shoebox on a shelf at the top. *Aha! Private papers.* Tamlyn couldn't reach the box, but she found an expandable walking stick from the backpack on the floor that she used to knock it off the shelf.

The top flew off the shoebox, and papers and letters spilled out over the floor. Tamlyn quickly gathered them up and placed them on the bed. She saw Professor von Telleman's teaching credentials, a few photographs of places she didn't recognize, and a book with chemical formulas. Then she saw an old handwritten letter in the original envelope, with no stamps or return address.

Tamlyn carefully pulled the fragile letter from the envelope to see it was signed "Viktoria." *That's my mother's name.* As she read the letter, she was astonished by the similarities to her own mother's story. *Could this letter have been written by my mother?*

She knew that her mother had fled from an abusive relationship, but her past was rarely discussed during her childhood. But the letter was written to the Professor, addressed as "my son." *I don't have a brother! Do I?*

Tamlyn never imagined that her mother had been married before or had other children. But if she was putting these pieces together correctly, that meant Professor von Telleman was her half-brother.

The realization hit Tamlyn like a blow to the stomach. *What happened to him? Mom left him with an abusive father? How could she do that?* Tamlyn hadn't studied much psychology, but she could imagine how terrible his life must have been. *Why didn't she take her son with her?* The only reason she could think of was that it would have been easier for her to hide alone. She even mentioned in her letter how she thought the man might track her down and kill her.

Tamlyn's head was spinning. She didn't know how long she had been sitting there, but suddenly she received a text from M'gera.

Are you okay? Did you find anything? When will you be finished?

Thank goodness! M'gera was checking in with her. Tamlyn felt her stomach settle. But her world was suddenly upside-down. She sent a quick text back.

Yes! I have to put some things back the way I found them. I'll be out in around ten minutes.

Tamlyn took a picture of the letter, hoping it was not too dark for the information to be seen. She carefully replaced the letters and other documents in the shoebox. She stood on a sturdy trash can that she moved from the kitchen to replace the box in the closet. She quickly replaced the can, then she went through the rooms to make sure everything else was as she had first found it. Then she went out the back door to meet M'gera by the boulder near the stream.

When Tamlyn recovered enough to return to her natural coloring, M'gera gasped when she saw her. "Tamlyn! You look terrible! Are you all right? Sit down."

Tamlyn shook her head and tried to gather her wits about her. She didn't want to explain about the letter she found, knowing they needed to get going.

"I think I found what we need. He ... I ... Let's go back to the facility so we can give the information to Nick and Hannah." Tamlyn felt like she wanted to fade into the background and disappear. But no matter how she felt, she knew that it was not over for her.

M'gera pulled her into a strong embrace. "Close your eyes. Take some deep breaths. Feel the strength of the mountain beneath you, feel the gentle rain on your face, and feel my compassion flowing into you. I'm here with you. You're a brave young woman. And I am proud of you."

"Thank you," Tamlyn said, resting her head on M'gera's shoulder, then she lifted her head and smiled.

Chapter 27: Preparation

Hannah, Nick, Olivia, and Lei Chen were gathered in the ground floor conference room of the Admin building, seated around a large oval table. Stephen joined via Zoom. They listened to M'gera and Tamlyn share the findings of Tamlyn's search of the cabin with incredulity.

Poor Tamlyn, finding out Gustav is her half-brother this way, Hannah thought. *Now it's up to us to act. We must find evidence—enough evidence to get him away from the project.*

"Okay. Let's figure this out," Hannah said. "Tamlyn and M'gera, I'd like you to keep watching the cabin in shifts with Tomas. Don't interact with Professor von Telleman. If you see him go into the cabin, take a picture. It's more evidence for us." Hannah watched for their reactions.

M'gera said, "I think Tomas and I can handle it. Now it would be better for Tamlyn to talk with Teani." M'gera smiled at her. "Really Tamlyn, Teani understands feelings better than anyone here. Talk with her, and you'll feel better."

Tamlyn nodded.

"I'll take her over to Teani's room," M'gera said.

"Thank you, M'gera," Hannah said. "Lei Chen will get in touch with you and Tomas later for your assignments." She waited until they left the room before she continued.

Olivia spoke up before Hannah got started. "It's fairly obvious that Tamlyn could be the target of Gustav's deviltry. We just don't know how his mind works. But from Adisa's reaction to him, I'm sure that his response will be violent."

"What makes you say that, Olivia?" Hannah croaked out the question.

"Stephen and I looked up some of Gustav's patents after he submitted the list of Class A chemicals he wanted for his classes. There were so many that we spent twenty-four hours researching his patents from the past eight years. He is a chemical genius, specializing in destruction. He has invented some very powerful chemical compounds; some of them even dissolve metal. He also has pending patents for two different neurotoxins. We've given him excuses why his chemical order cannot be filled, but he doesn't have to order dangerous drugs. He can create them." Olivia spat the words out as if they were poison.

Come on, Robert, Hannah thought. *Lend me some of that strength you found when disasters got in your way.* "We can do this if we each take on one aspect of his activities. Lei Chen, I'd like you to review his contract to see if there is anything we can use to fire him. Stephen, I want you to find out who owns that cabin Gustav is using. One thing's for sure, he never got our permission to use it." Lei Chen and Stephen nodded, writing notes on their computer tablets.

"Nick, I'd like you to talk with Benito, the construction worker Adisa identified, to see if he has been working with Gustav. But first, check with foreman Mateo. He might have more information as well. Now for James and Maya: I'd like the two of you to work with the children to expand their understanding of each other. When I passed one of the classrooms yesterday, I heard children arguing. The teacher started laughing, and the children calmed down. Conflict between the children is starting. I was wondering if you two had any ideas about how we could handle this," Hannah asked. *It's important to keep the children calm and focused on learning.*

James looked thoughtful. "Isn't that part of the classroom experience? Conflicting points of view are discussed to better understand the subject?"

"We need a different approach for XL-ENCE. Because mutual respect and cooperation are fundamental to solving problems, it must start early in development. The children can experience this in the classroom, where they are outside of the family unit. They must feel bonds with people they don't really know yet to let understanding in. How would you approach it?" Hannah asked.

James smiled at Hannah and said, "I first look at the tools that are available. For example, if everyone in a group loves ice cream, I would start with that. For these special children, I might start with something like caring for an injured puppy or kitten. Children have natural compassion for animal babies. But their approaches to helping the animals might produce some interesting results. I know that Chelsea would sing or play a song on her flute to help the animal be calm in her presence. Another child would likely take a different approach."

"That's what we need. How could we have missed how much we need a class like that? Can you come up with some tasks for the children to work on together that will help them share ideas? I bet the Accelerators could use a few lessons as well. But we can leave that to Lei Chen and Teani," Hannah explained.

Maya ran her hands through her blonde curls. "If we use an environmental focus, we can plant a garden and have the children care for the plants. Wouldn't Grams and Grandpa Neil be thrilled to see that happening here?"

Hannah breathed a sigh of relief. "Genius! Last of all, Olivia. I would like you and David to set up the drones to monitor and record the cabin and the entire northwest side of the mountain up to the Bridge to Forever. And don't use lights—it would be too obvious. Use the most photosensitive equipment you can find. Let me know when you test it out. I'd like to see the images that come in."

Olivia rubbed her palms together. "Good. I was hoping to get in on the tech end of this operation. That's one of David's strongest skill areas. We'll get right on it." The group dispersed, eager to tackle their assigned tasks.

✦ ✦ ✦

Lei Chen pulled up Gustav's contract to see if there had been any significant changes to the standard language set up by the lawyers. Access to his business accounts from the project computers was negotiated for a period of one year. After that, he would have to buy his own computer to access his accounts.

Then he found the "Grounds for Termination" section, which said, "Immoral or unprofessional conduct; commission, aiding, or advocating the commission of acts of a criminal nature; dishonesty; unsatisfactory performance; evident unfitness for service; physical or mental condition unfitting him or her to instruct or associate with children; persistent violation of or refusal to obey state or federal laws; conviction of a felony; and alcoholism or other drug abuse that makes the employee unfit to instruct or associate with children."

Hannah's right. We need evidence and most of it relates to that cabin. Tomas and I will take the first observation shift. He called Tomas and arranged for them to meet at 5 a.m. in the picnic area before heading up the mountain.

Early the next morning, Lei Chen gave Tomas one of his cameras, and he took his Canon with the larger telescoping lens to take pictures of the activities around the cabin. Tomas would be on the western side, near the stream where there was plenty of cover. Lei Chen would be on the southern side, hidden behind some large rocks and fallen trees.

They both saw Gustav boiling leaves and roots in a small pot on an outdoor propane camp stove. He placed some of the concoction into a bird feeder with water on one side and seed on the other. He hung the feeder from a tree near the north side of the cabin where he could observe the effects on the birds, who were quick to swoop in as soon as Gustav moved out of the way. It was no more than five minutes before the birds stopped feeding and drinking and fell off the feeder onto the ground. Gustav retrieved two of the birds and took them into the cabin.

Lei Chen sent a quick text to Tomas:

Do you have anything with you that you can use to get a sample of the liquid in that bird feeder?

Tomas sent a quick text back:

Hold on. I'll check.

A few minutes later he texted:

I had a pill bottle in my backpack. I washed it out. I can use that. Can you make some noise to distract him when I get close to the pot?

Lei Chen wondered, *How to distract him? I can try shaking some of these fallen tree branches. That should make enough noise to draw him out of the other side of the cabin.*

He texted back to Tomas:

I will make some noise with the tree branches and try to stay hidden. Let me know when you are almost there.

Lei Chen took off his glasses to wipe away the sweat that started to drip down into his eyes. He looked around at the tree branches, searching for ones that were very dry and might break easily. The previous day's rain had soaked most of the wood, but he spotted some dry branches underneath the pile. He took his camera and moved it to a spot farther down the mountain. When he returned to the fallen trees, he could see Tomas moving slowly toward the north side of the cabin.

Tomas texted:

I'm ready.

Lei Chen gritted his teeth and pulled sharply on the dry branches. Some of the large, wetter branches started rolling down the hill. He stood on the dry branches, exerting his weight to break them. The larger ones cracked apart with a loud snap. Just as Gustav came out of the front door of the cabin, Lei Chen fell backward over one of the fallen trees. He put a hand over his mouth because he was breathing hard and didn't want to be heard.

Gustav took a few steps toward Lei Chen's hiding place. Lei Chen crouched lower, glad that his brown jacket blended so well with the wet trees.

Gustav was standing very still now. *He would be foolish to be caught out here. How could he explain it?*

Lei Chen watched as Tomas silently crept up to the back of the cabin. Using his gloved hand, Tomas dipped the pill container into the pot of the bird feeder, pulled it out, then screwed on the lid. He placed the container into a leather pouch at his waist.

Tomas sent another text:

I'm done. Heading back to the stream.

Thank goodness! Lei Chen thought. He texted:

> Stay there. Be careful with that glove. Don't touch it! Turn it inside out and keep it with the pill bottle. Wait for Gustav to go back inside. Give him ten minutes, then we can start down. Be as quiet as you can.

It took them another ninety minutes to get back to the project. Then it would be M'gera's turn to see if more evidence could be gathered in.

Chapter 28: A Dangerous Plan

The next day, the Management Team met in Hannah's sunlit office to review the results of their investigations.

First, Nick reported, "Mateo said that Gustav asked him for maps of the mountain area to plan his hiking routes. However, Benito said that he had been helping Gustav move boxes of supplies to the cabin in the forest. When I asked him what the supplies were, Benito said he didn't know, but that Gustav had warned him to be careful because some of the things inside were breakable. He became ill in the cabin after the job was done."

Stephen was next. "The New Zealand Forestry Service has cabins in the mountain regions throughout the entire island. Cabins that were abandoned during the pandemic have remained vacant, for the most part. None of the vacant cabins are available for use by the public or businesses. It's likely that Gustav is using one of those."

Lei Chen confirmed Stephen's guess. "I sent the pictures I took yesterday to Sarah Dowie, who sent them on to her government contacts. They confirmed that it's a Forestry Service cabin. According to the contract termination clause in Gustav's contract, his use of the cabin would fall under 'violation of or refusal to obey state and federal laws.' But the 'immoral or unprofessional conduct' clause would be much more effective for terminating him. We just need more evidence of where the supplies in his cabin came from and what his intent is."

Hannah listened quietly, and when the conversation died down, she stood. "I have a terrible feeling that we are going to have to draw him out. We need a plan to make him act before he is ready. He is too good at covering his tracks. We can hide the plan inside a Challenge for the children. If the Challenge includes a hike up the mountain, with Tamlyn participating, I think he would jump at the chance to act, if we are right that she is his target."

Hannah continued, "I want to have more adults involved in this Challenge as protection for the children. Lei Chen and Teani will act as leads for two teams; one will go up the east side of the mountain, the other will go up the west side. Tomas, Nicholai, Logan, and I will accompany the groups as observers. Olivia and David will control the drones, filming the teams throughout the Challenge. Most of our Challenges take two or three days, and we probably want to stick to that format to draw Gustav in. We will let the teachers and the Accelerators know about the Challenge, of course, but only we will know about the plan to capture Gustav in the act. Are there any questions?"

Lei Chen spoke first. "You realize that we're putting Tamlyn in terrible danger to draw him out. What chance do any of us have of stopping him?"

"Tamlyn must know the full plan, and Enrique and Hahona as well. All of us will be there to stop

Gustav," Hannah asserted. "No one will be farther away from her than twenty feet. Lei Chen, can you and Teani get the Challenge together? Logan and Tomas can prepare the supplies. Nick, please put information about the Challenge on the website for everyone to see tonight."

Maya and James had been very quiet, so Hannah said, "Maya, you and James will be working with the children and teachers here. Is there anything you want to say about the plan?"

"I have two concerns," Maya said. "The first is whether or not Gustav has a weapon. It might not be a gun, but he's sure to have a hunting knife if he spent his life hiking and camping in forested areas. We think he might be planning to use drugs, but if he feels like he's being hunted, he could resort to physical violence, too. James was trained in the military to combat knife assailants, and I think he should spend some time training Tamlyn as soon as possible."

"That's a very good idea. Thank you, Maya. And your second concern?"

"I think we need to tell Father Brennan, Sister Angelique, and Sarah about this plan. Someone could die on this Challenge! If we want their support, if this plan really goes south, they must be informed." Maya gazed thoughtfully at Hannah. "I know I'm the liaison, but I think this should come from you, Hannah."

This is all happening so damn fast! But Maya is right. Our contacts need to be told. What do I tell them? We found a fox in the hen house? Father

Brennan warned me about this, so I should talk to him first.

"I will make some calls tonight," Hannah said, and then she turned to Lei Chen and asked, "Has the sample Tomas got from the bird feeder at the cabin been analyzed yet?"

"No. Because we have no other chemists here, we had to send it to Queenstown for analysis. It might take a few more days before we get any results," he told them.

"Olivia, the entire Management Team will be involved in the Challenge in one way or another. Can you ask Amanda to keep checking for the chemical analysis results to come in? That will provide more evidence of what he's planning," Hannah said.

"Sure, Hannah. This won't be easy for Amanda though. She recruited Tamlyn in Austria, and Tamlyn has been confiding in her since she got here. She'll be as worried as the rest of us—if not more," Olivia noted.

James stood and said, "Listen up, people. Basically, this is a war council. We all understand the risks. And we don't have much time to prepare. I'm going to pull Amanda, M'gera, and Tamlyn into the gym right now for hand-to-hand combat training. We need to inform Tamlyn about the Challenge and the secret plan. We'll do our best to help her face her fears. Learning to protect herself will give her more confidence. It may take all night for everyone to feel confident in their skills, so let them sleep in tomorrow. I'll text you all when we're done." James kissed Maya, holding her face between his hands and looking into her eyes for a full minute. Then he sighed and left the conference room.

✦ ✦ ✦

Father Brennan answered Hannah's call on the third ring. "Hello there, Miss Hannah. What'll you be needing at this late hour?" he asked.

"I need to tell you about a problem we are facing at XL-ENCE," Hannah said without preamble. "We believe that one of our teachers has made a paralytic solution from one of the native plants. We have proof that he has been experimenting on birds in the forest. We have photos of him illegally staying in an abandoned Forestry Service cabin. He has an entire secret lab set up in that cabin. We are gravely concerned about what he might be planning to do next." Hannah paused to give Father Brennan the chance to process that shocking information.

"Hannah, no wonder you sound so worried," the Father said.

"It gets worse," Hannah continued. "We discovered that the Professor is the half-brother of one of our staff members, an assistant Accelerator named Tamlyn. She had no idea she even had a half-brother. She found an old letter that was written to him by their mother. When we read it, we learned that their mother abandoned the Professor when he was just a boy and left him with his abusive father. The Professor hasn't approached the young woman about it yet, and maybe we are jumping to conclusions here, but we fear that he might be plotting to harm her.

"I remember the warning you gave me about darkness being drawn in where the light is bright," Hannah said. "It scared me to death when I heard you say it." Hannah ran out of breath, forcing the story out and wondering what Father Brennan would say.

"And why are you calling me?" Father Brennan asked. "Prayers are not going to help now. Now is the time for action. What are you going to do?"

Right to the point. I better tell him the whole plan, Hannah thought, and then she outlined the plan to draw Gustav out with Tamlyn as bait during a Challenge prepared for the students on the mountain. The hope was that the adults and Tamlyn would pass by the cabin Gustav was using, and then he would follow Tamlyn.

"Why on Earth haven't you contacted the police?" Father Brennan asked.

"We don't have enough evidence of what he's planning to get him arrested by law enforcement," Hannah explained. "The Forestry Service would have to press charges to evict him from the cabin, and we only told them about it today. We have one day to prepare. Tamlyn is being trained in hand-to-hand combat, and the whole Challenge will be filmed via drones. I'd like to hear your thoughts." Hannah's stomach was in knots.

Father Brennan was quiet. Hannah imagined him praying, as he had done when they had lunch. "I wish I could tell you that everything will be alright. But you know better. You have a good plan. Stick to it. You're right. Evidence is what you need. I'll tell Sister Angelique what's going on. Combating evil is never easy. At least you recognized it early. We're ready to assist if you need us," he told her.

"Thank you, Father Brennan. We'll do everything we can to protect Tamlyn. I have to admit that I'm afraid of Gustav, but I think I am angrier that he might be planning to hurt that sweet young lady."

"Let your anger give you strength. Let your love give you hope. God be with you, child." Father Brennan gave Hannah his blessing and then hung up.

Amen, Hannah thought.

Chapter 29: Gustav and Hannah

When Gustav retrieved two of the birds that drank the distilled taraonga, he wanted to see how long it would take for them to either recover or die. Bird metabolism was much faster than human metabolism, yet it was close to twenty-five minutes before the birds started to move their wings.

He was preparing to concentrate the mixture when a notice bell alerted him to a new posting on the XL-ENCE website. He read about the new Challenge for the students and Accelerators that would begin in two days and pass by the cabin on their way to the Bridge to Forever. *Damn! There is no time to test the drug on mammals before the Challenge begins. How can I get the toxin into Tamlyn? As a gesture of support, I can give her a thermos of iced tea. She won't know it is laced with a strong dose of the drug. As she climbs the mountain to reach the Bridge to Forever, her metabolism will increase delivery of the drug to her muscles. Paralysis should set in by the time she reaches the top.*

As a scientist and businessman, Gustav routinely developed contingency plans. He wanted the fallback plan to mimic the death he planned for Tamlyn, so that he could watch her falling from the bridge. For Plan B, he used one of his patented chemicals that dissolved metals. He sold it to quarry companies to extract metals from rock and soil material. He barely had enough to place some in plastic containers to secure to the underside of the bridge. *When she crosses the bridge, I can trigger the release mechanism. The drone I took from the supply center will allow me to watch Tamlyn as the bridge dissolves beneath her. They will have to cross the bridge as part of the Challenge.*

Gustav woke early the morning before the Challenge would begin to get to his supplies at the cabin. First, he hiked to the Bridge to Forever to secure the containers of metal-dissolving chemical and the release triggers. He climbed a tree about halfway between the cabin and the bridge to hide the drone he would use. He would be able to see the students and Accelerators, especially Tamlyn, anywhere along the path. Then Gustav hurried back to his classroom, with his heart pounding in anticipation of the events that would play out the next day.

✦✦✦

It was close to 8 that morning when Hannah requested a short conference with Lei Chen. He was stocking his backpack when Hannah knocked on the door of his apartment.

"Come in," he said.

"I have something for you to take into the Challenge," Hannah said as she walked to the couch. "This device is called a SonoPrep. It was invented by our benefactor, Robert Langer. It produces sonic waves that allow medication and other fluids to penetrate the skin painlessly. It can also be used to remove toxins, but they will need to be washed off the skin once they have been extracted. I want you to take it with us in case we need to treat an injury in the forest." She paused and took a breath.

"I think there is more to this," he said, watching Hannah's face. "It's about the danger we face from Gustav. Do you know if it works?"

"This device has been used all over the world for many years to remove toxins like snake venom as well as to give medicines," she replied. "We strongly suspect he will try to give the paralyzing agent to the forest team. I don't know how he'll do it, but we must be very careful around him and the cabin he's using. As you know, other chemical compounds he's invented are just as dangerous."

Lei Chen nodded. "We must face the fact that he may be a killer. Thank you for the SonoPrep. It's best to be prepared. How do you use it?"

Hannah quickly demonstrated how the device works and then clasped her hands together to keep them from shaking. "There is more. I'm going to pull Gustav out of class today and fire him. Nick will be with me in case Gustav gets violent, but I expect him to be very stoic about it. I'll give him four hours to pack and get out. David will be watching him. If he goes to the airport and gets on a plane, we might be rid of him until he tries to sue us for breaking his contract. But it's more likely that he'll make it appear as if he's leaving but will circle back to the cabin and wait for the Challenge to begin tomorrow." Hannah felt the tears starting but rubbed them away. Her tension and fear were becoming more difficult to keep in check. And now she would be forced into a personal confrontation with Gustav.

✦ ✦ ✦

At 10 a.m., Gustav saw Hannah approaching his classroom during a break between his classes. *Oh no! What does she want now?* He stepped away from his desk and waited for her to enter his domain. When Hannah didn't open the door, he saw her through the door window, waving for him to come out into the hallway. *So, I must go to her. Time to play the compliant teacher.*

"Good morning, Ms. Larsen. What can I do for you today?" Gustav asked in a light, bantering tone. Gustav was surprised when he looked at her face. He remembered seeing that look of anger on his father's face when he was a small boy, frightened of the dark, seeking help. His heart dropped into his stomach.

"Professor von Telleman, you are hereby terminated from your position with our project. You have four hours to pack your *personal* effects and exit the grounds. If you wish, we will provide you with an escort into Queenstown or to the airport. Your access has been blocked to the project's website and all buildings other than your rooms in the staff building." Hannah crossed her arms, waiting for him to reply.

That bitch! Who does she think she is? You can't get rid of me that easily. "Excuse me, upon what grounds are you basing this firing decision?

It is my right to know," Gustav said, barely holding his anger inside.

"We won't be discussing that with you at this time," Hannah said, reaching into the pocket of her blue blazer. "But here is the card for our legal firm. You're welcome to contact them with any complaints you have. Mr. Resenden will escort you to your rooms."

The previous night, Nick had informed the lawyers about their decision to fire Gustav. He explained that the reasons were too complex to explain over the phone, but that they had collected evidence to support taking this step. Nick told Hannah that the lawyers said they would be prepared to respond to any legal action Gustav might initiate.

Gustav hadn't noticed Nick standing behind Hannah in the hallway. He was taller than Gustav, well-muscled and fit. Gustav felt his fists clenching. *How would you like me to smash your face in?* But was it worth it? He was so close to his revenge. If he acted out violently, he'd end up in jail. *YOU CAN'T STOP ME. I will go away now and come back tonight.* He spoke through clenched teeth, "Very well. I will call for transportation after I have finished packing."

The venom in Gustav's voice caused Hannah to back up a few steps. But she stood firm as Nick walked with him out of the Education building. *Now, I must talk with Tamlyn,* Hannah thought as she pulled out her phone and called Maya. "Hello Maya. How are you, sister mine? Is James still sleeping?" she asked.

"Hi, Hannah. James is taking a shower. You know him. It doesn't matter if he's up all night; he's always ready to go in the morning. I'm holding it together for Bobby and Chelsea. They always keep me grounded. What do you need?"

"I should talk to Tamlyn. Do you know where she is?"

"Hmmm. I would check the staff dormitory first. She's probably still asleep," Maya said.

I doubt it, Hannah thought. *She might have more confidence after her self-defense lessons, but she's probably still more afraid than any of us can imagine.* "Thanks, Maya. I won't be long. I'll check in with you both after lunch."

Hannah walked slowly to the staff dormitory. She stood outside Tamlyn's door, ready to knock, when the door flew open before her. Tamlyn stood, framed by the light coming from the window behind her. She was dressed in jeans, a white T-shirt, and a tie-dyed turquoise-and-pink hoodie. But it was her face that stopped Hannah from speaking. She looked so calm!

"Oh, Hannah! I umm ... was just going to get some food. I'm starving," Tamlyn said.

I bet she is. "This will only take a few minutes. Could we talk in your room?"

Tamlyn nodded, walked over to her bed, and sat down. "You can sit on the desk chair. It's not very comfortable though."

Hannah sat next to her on the bed. "I fired Gustav this morning. He's packing up right now. I've given him another target—me—so you don't have to participate in the Challenge. I wanted you to know." She ran out of words, watching Tamlyn think about what she said.

Tamlyn started shaking her head. A lopsided smile appeared on her face as her wavy blonde hair caressed her cheeks. "I want to do this. You might not understand my reasons, but I feel like I need to give him a chance to become my brother, not my enemy. Maybe if he sees me hiking in the forest, the way he has done so many times, he might feel a connection that will stop him from wanting to hurt me."

Hannah was speechless. *Who is this amazing girl? Poor Gustav. He never knew her.* "Are you sure about this?"

Tamlyn looked solemnly at Hannah. "Yes. Everyone deserves a chance to become a better person."

Chapter 30: The Eastside Mountain Challenge

Olivia tasked Logan with preparing the supplies for the teams working on the mountain to lure Gustav into the open. The younger children, Hahona and Enrique, would have skill Challenges to resolve on their way up the mountain. However, they were also aware of the potential danger once they reached the Bridge to Forever. Logan not only felt the fears presented by the Management Team, but felt himself pulling inward as he usually did when danger surrounded him, a holdover survival mechanism he developed during his childhood in Ireland. Now, the responsibility to prepare the supplies to keep the teams safe pressed against his chest like heavy weights. He pulled out his phone to call for help.

"Hi, Amanda. I am prepping the packs and camping gear. Can you come over to the supply building to help? We need to figure out how to divide everything so that the teams can carry the load," Logan explained.

"Do you think we could get a donkey or mule to help carry some of the heavier gear? We often use them in Australia for rough terrain or longer trips," Amanda suggested.

"I have no idea, but probably not. Please try to get over here as soon as you can. We should try to split up everything on the list first. Then fill the packs. If there is gear left over, we can think about other alternatives."

Amanda felt like Logan was ordering her around as if she were his employee. *I can't let him get away with that!*

"Logan, do you realize that you are talking to me like you are my boss? We're supposed to be mates. You're not even considering my suggestions! I'm just as qualified as you are to handle these tasks," Amanda fired back at him.

Logan felt like he had been slapped. He was only telling her what was needed to get the job done. But ... he didn't listen to her. She was just another pair of hands to him right now. Dammit! Those old habits came out when he was under pressure. Amanda deserved an apology.

"Amanda, I'm sorry that I talked to you that way. It's an old habit that I have been trying to break for a long time. When I am stressed, I feel like I can't rely on anyone but myself. And I hate asking for help. I would appreciate it if you'd give me another chance. I guess I'm more stressed out about this whole plan than I thought," Logan said.

Amanda realized that she had spoken up to defend herself against one of the strongest Accelerators. Maybe he was good for her. "I will. I guess I'm pumped up from the self-defense training we had last night. But next time, I might punch back instead of talking."

Logan laughed hard and so did Amanda. "See you later," they said together.

✦ ✦ ✦

Teani told Logan to hike up toward the Bridge to Forever. He could start preparing the camp for where they were planning to spend the night. She would be working with the students to use their skills in the forest. Nick would follow them as an observer and warn them of any dangers from behind.

She led Enrique and Hahona up the southeast path away from the project site after checking their packs against the supply list. Nick followed closely behind. This would be a two-day hike, and they would sleep overnight in a sheltered area or cave, depending on what they found. Both boys were eager to help protect Tamlyn; they saw her as the big sister they never had. Their path led to the eastern edge of the Bridge to Forever. Teani knew there were several opportunities for them to learn about the flora and fauna of the forest, strengthening their natural talents. They had been hiking for about sixty minutes when she called a stop to hydrate and get their bearings.

"What can you tell me about the forest so far?" Teani asked.

Enrique pushed his blond-brown hair back and focused his attention outward. "There are two birds' nests in the trees above us. One has three eggs in it; the other has two eggs. The baby birds will be hatching soon, maybe in a couple of weeks. If you listen, you can hear the parents scolding us because we are too close. Where are the wolves, big cats, or even wild dogs? I don't feel any predators around here."

Teani nodded. "That is a very good question, Enrique. Our native guides told us that New Zealand split away from other land masses before there were any native mammal predators. The smaller species were left to evolve without those hunters. And, in order to preserve the native animals, no predators have been introduced by man."

"I have a lot to learn about New Zealand. It's so different from Brazil," Enrique said.

"How about you, Hahona? What have you noticed?"

"The trees here produce a lot of seeds, and there are bushes and vines for berries, which provide food for the birds and smaller animals," Hahona said. "A lot of the smells are new to me. Some are musty and others are sharp. I think the musty smells come from the forest floor. The sharp smells are from broken stems and some flower shoots. There are so many different plants here from the area where I grew up. Are any of them used as medicines?"

"You can take some samples if you wear your gloves and pack them in the containers in your container kit," Teani said. "Consider it part of the Challenge for you to determine what uses can be made from the plants. You are both doing very well. But we need to go farther into the forest. Are you ready? Check your packs and remember to drink some water every twenty minutes."

After consulting the map, Teani led them directly west. They stopped two hours later to refill their water containers and eat lunch. A stream tumbled noisily down the mountain side. The water was cold, clear, and refreshing. Hahona finished his lunch first and asked, "Teani, may I hike along the stream to look for interesting plants and flowers?"

"It is dangerous to hike where water makes rocks slippery and loose," Teani reminded him.

"I'll be careful. I promise," Hahona told her. "I will return within fifteen minutes."

Enrique waved him on his way, with his mouth full of fruit from their lunch.

It was time to check in with Lei Chen. "Hello," Teani whispered. "We are about 30 percent of the way up. No problems for us; the boys are doing well. Logan is hiking further up to start setting up the overnight camp. Nick is observing, leaving most of the leadership direction to me. How is your group doing?"

"Hi, Teani. We are okay. Tomas has been very brave trying to make Gustav aware of our presence on his side of the mountain. We are still too close to him to talk freely, so let's try to keep our communications via text. Next check-in is four hours away at sunset. Take care."

"As they say: 10-4," Teani replied and cut off.

When Hahona returned from his hike, Teani and Enrique were cleaning up the area. He showed them a beautiful plant with yellow flowers, some moss that was almost iridescent, and a few insects.

"I haven't paid much attention to plants," Enrique said. "Thanks, Hahona. This is very interesting. How is the other team doing, Teani?"

"They are fine, trying to keep their climb quiet and unobtrusive. Do you know what that word means?" Teani asked. Nick smiled as he waited for the boys to answer.

"In the background," Hahona said.

"Not noticeable," Enrique replied.

"Yes, you are both correct. We will meet up with them at the Bridge to Forever. Now, we will continue our exploration by walking along the stream for a little while as it moves north," Teani said. "Don't forget to take pictures to share with the staff and other children."

Hahona packed up his samples and led them north. Twenty minutes later, Enrique stopped and motioned to the others to stand still. "There is a hurt animal nearby," he said softly. "I feel little prickles in my hands when I sense an animal in pain. This one is about the size of a small deer. I think the pain is near its hind leg." He motioned for the others to squat down. "When I was a small boy, it was really confusing. I wasn't sure what was happening to me. My sister realized that I was sensing when our neighbor's cat started having babies. She helped me to separate my own feelings from others I was sensing."

"Are there any other animals nearby?" Teani whispered.

Enrique shook his head. "I don't sense anything but birds. We really should go find it. It needs our help."

Teani was worried about how the animal might react. "Before we go, I want you to tell us more about the animal. Is it hungry? Thirsty? Young or old? Can it move at all? Is it bleeding? Take some time, go deeper. We need to protect ourselves as well as help the animal."

"Okay," Enrique said impatiently. "Can I use the metronome application on my phone? I will try to match the animal's heartbeat first, then slow it down as we move closer," he explained.

"Where did you learn about that technique, Enrique?" Nick asked.

"It's like when babies are afraid or hurt, their heartbeat speeds up. Their mother soothes it by holding the baby close to her chest. Her heartbeat calms the baby and tells the baby it is safe. When the baby calms down, the mother can find out what's wrong faster."

"I never realized that. Thank you for explaining it to me," Nick said.

"Do you need to see the animal to calm it?" Hahona whispered.

"I will feel when the animal's heartbeat matches the beat of the metronome. Once it is calmer, I will slowly come out of the brush so that it can see me before we approach it. I will gather more information as we get closer," Enrique said.

Teani thought about what to do and said, "Okay. Let's start the metronome and see if the animal can hear it. You can move closer to be sure. We'll start slowly and then adjust as the information comes in. How does that sound?"

Hahona pointed to the stream and said, "Let me pull some of these plants near the stream. They might help to soothe the animal's pain or may be good to eat if the animal is hungry. Some mosses are used to slow bleeding. It would be good to gather some, just in case. Other animals might be drawn to the injured animal if it is bleeding."

"Remember, there are no predatory animals in this forest," Teani said. "But let's be careful.

If it's a young animal, it might call for its mother, who might see us as a threat. Enrique, start the metronome now and start moving toward the animal."

Enrique took the lead, pulling them to the northwest. After a few minutes, he began to whisper. "I think it's a young goat! They are very skilled at climbing up and down mountains."

"What else can you sense from it? Keep going and explain as the information becomes clear to you," Teani directed.

Enrique kept walking toward the goat, slowing the pulse of the metronome as he drew nearer. "It is thirsty. The pain comes in waves. It keeps trying to stand up and falling back down." Teani, Nick, and Hahona crept slowly along behind Enrique.

"Stop! I can see it," Enrique said, then he slowly emerged from the brush, crouching down to appear smaller and less frightening. The others weren't far behind, but they stayed hidden in the brush. Enrique calmed his own heartbeat. The goat looked at Enrique crawling toward it. It started struggling to stand, but it quickly fell back down. Enrique crawled closer, holding out his hands. Enrique's green eyes focused on the goat. When the goat let out a small bleat, he moved to its side, hovering his hands above its hindquarters. He motioned for Hahona to approach.

Hahona took a pan from Teani's pack and poured some water into it. Then he placed it by the goat's head. It was awkward, but the goat was able to slurp up some of the water by turning its head and forelegs. Enrique noted the swollen area and searched for other injuries along the leg. Hahona watched as Enrique checked the goat and breathed a sigh of relief when no blood was detected.

"Try putting some of the streamside plants on this area," Enrique said as he pointed to the swollen area. "He is calm and will not kick or bite us."

Teani grabbed her camera and started recording the boys treating the goat. Enrique talked to the goat in his soft, gentle voice. "I can't feel anything like a broken bone. I think it's just a bad sprain," Enrique said. "He is young and will probably heal pretty fast."

"So it's a male goat?" Hahona asked.

"That's the feeling I get from him," Enrique said. "He is old enough to be away from his mother. What I know about young goats is that they start jumping very early. They even jump onto the backs of adult goats. This is practice for climbing up rocky areas. This goat might have been jumping to a place where the ground was ... um, crumbly, causing him to twist around and try to land on his feet."

Teani watched as the boys took care of the goat. "The goat seems to be glad we're here. Reducing pain is the first priority. Now, you need to think ahead. What else should we be doing to help him?"

"He needs a quiet place to heal up for a day or two. We should look for a place where we can leave him with some food and water. I think he will stay put until he can get around on his own," Enrique said.

"I can scout a little further up the trail," Hahona offered. "If I don't find anything in twenty minutes,

I will come back here and then try a different direction."

"If you find a good place for him further up, how will we move him uphill?" Teani asked.

Hahona thought about it for a couple of minutes. "If it's not too far away, we could put him on the blankets in our packs and drag him."

"I can help, too," Nick said. "We can switch off if one of you gets tired."

Hahona nodded. "I'd better get going."

Teani reminded him to call or return. Night could fall quickly in the forest, and she didn't want them to try moving the goat in the dark. Enrique sat with his hands above the goat's hindquarters, concentrating with his eyes closed and breathing deeply.

Nick texted Lei Chen with a brief description of what was happening with the group, then asked about Tamlyn.

Lei Chen texted:

We are okay for now. Tomas is watching the cabin. We expect Gustav to follow us as we get further up the mountain. Keep in touch. Don't call unless it's an emergency.

"How are you feeling, Enrique?" Teani asked.

"I'm getting a little tired from staying in one position. Could I have some water? I want to make sure the pain level is down before I move away."

Teani held her canteen to his lips and tipped it up gently so he could drink. Then she unwrapped an energy bar and fed it to him in small chunks.

She remained standing so that she could scout the area while Enrique was sitting down. Twenty minutes flew by quickly. She was starting to get concerned when Hahona texted:

> I found a place that will work. It's not too far up the hill. There are droopy tree branches and leaves to hide him. If we keep the goat calm, you or Nick can collect some food for him as we go.

Teani showed Enrique the text.

"Let's get the goat onto the blanket. Then we can take off as soon as Hahona gets back," Enrique said.

"Nick and I will follow behind you, getting food for the goat." She took a deep breath. "You have both done very well. We need to get the goat settled before it starts getting dark. Then we can camp for the night. Logan has set up the overnight area for us. We will continue toward the Bridge to Forever tomorrow."

Chapter 31: The Westside Mountain Challenge

Tamlyn, Tomas, Hannah, and Lei Chen walked along the northwest path marked on the map. Tomas took the point position so that he could observe activity in and around the cabin. He removed the binoculars from his pack, setting them up to hide any reflection from the lenses. He motioned for Lei Chen and Tamlyn to move farther up the path. Hannah stayed behind, further to the west of where Tomas was stationed.

Tomas walked around to the forest area facing the front of the cabin, but stayed well back from view. He noticed that the windows were closed with the blinds shuttered—all except a small window next to the front door. Using the binoculars, Tomas could see inside. A small portion of the front room and the kitchen were visible, and Tomas could tell Gustav wasn't in those rooms. He pulled out his phone and texted what he had found to Lei Chen.

The return message was not what Tomas expected:

> Stay there. Tamlyn is coming to join you. Wait for her and let me know when she reaches you.

Tomas continued to watch the cabin intently for activity. He nearly screeched when Tamlyn suddenly appeared beside him.

"Sorry," she whispered. "I thought it would be better for you to see me than to touch you while I was camouflaged."

"It's okay," Tomas replied, wiping sweat from his forehead with his arm. "I should have remembered. This wasn't part of the plan we talked about this morning. What has changed?"

"Lei Chen wants you to knock on the cabin door and ask Professor von Telleman for directions to the nearest stream to fill your canteen. Be very careful. Whatever he says, don't go into the cabin with him," Tamlyn explained.

"I need to text back that you have arrived. Hold on." Tomas sent the message and waited for a response. "What are you doing here? Those instructions could have been texted to me."

"Lei Chen wants me to see if I can pick up some other information from around the cabin. Professor von Telleman won't see me in the shadows, so I will be safe as long as you distract him."

"I don't feel good about leaving you here, even if you're hidden," Tomas said. "Hannah won't be able to help you; she's too far away. What if something unexpected happens?"

"I'm not going inside the cabin or near the Professor. I'm just collecting data. It's not time to draw him out yet. Hannah and I will meet you at the next checkpoint."

Tomas shook his head. "I don't like it, but okay. You get going. When you fade from view, I'll knock on his door."

Tomas watched Tamlyn move into the shadows on the south side of the cabin. He emptied his canteen and then walked over to the cabin and knocked loudly on the door. He could hear movements inside. *Relax, you're just out for a hike and need some water. He doesn't know this part of the Challenge has changed.*

Gustav opened the door and eyed Tomas with surprise.

"So! You are one of the Accelerators. Yes?" he asked Tomas.

"Professor! I'm surprised to see you here. Excuse me, but I need to refill my canteen. Could you direct me to the nearest stream?"

Gustav looked at Tomas, keeping a neutral expression on his face. Tomas could see the suspicion in his eyes. He backed slightly away from the door. Gustav didn't respond but looked out around the front of the cabin.

"You are alone? With no maps? That does not seem very responsible," Gustav said. "I have not really explored much of this area myself. I think the nearest water source is southeast of here. Or you could return to the facility, of course. It is only about five miles from here."

Tomas kicked himself mentally for not thinking his situation out more thoroughly before talking with the Professor. He knew the project site was located southeast of the cabin. But he didn't want to go in that direction. "I see. Thank you, Professor. I was instructed to go north into the forest. So, I'll be going on my way."

"Wait!" Gustav said. "I can fill your canteen for you. Please wait here," he said while reaching for Tomas's canteen. "It won't take me long." When

Gustav walked through the swinging door, Tomas could see the kitchen.

"Thank you, Professor. That's very kind of you," Tomas called out to him.

Strangely, Tomas did not hear water streaming from the faucets. When Gustav returned, he handed the canteen back to Tomas. "Enjoy your hike. I hope you are successful."

Tomas waved goodbye and started north. It took him about forty-five minutes to reach the stream designated as the checkpoint. He drank from the stream, leaving the liquid in the canteen untouched. Lei Chen and Tamlyn called out to him a short while later.

"Tomas! Please tell me that you didn't drink from your canteen after the Professor filled it up!" Tamlyn cried.

"I didn't. Don't worry. When I didn't hear water coming from the faucets, I knew it probably wasn't safe," he said.

"I saw him pour it from a jug on the counter. He might have heard me as I went past the window. I saw him open the blinds and look around. He didn't close them all the way. That's when I saw what he did," Tamlyn said.

Hannah watched and listened as they discussed Gustav's actions. "Now he'll expect Tomas to become paralyzed. You'll either need to get way ahead of us or stay off to the sides to stay out of sight when he comes out." *More complications, just what we don't need right now.* "At least he's where we expected him to be," Hannah said.

"Put the canteen in my pack. You can use mine," Lei Chen said as he traded equipment with Tomas.

"Are we going to return to the original plan now?" Tamlyn asked.

Lei Chen looked at them and shook his head. "I'd like Tomas to circle back to the Professor's cabin and follow him when he leaves. Tamlyn, Hannah, and I will go northwest. We have to move slowly because he might have set traps along the path. Our next checkpoint is the cave about 600 feet below the Bridge to Forever. It is clearly marked on the map and was checked by M'gera early this morning. We can stay there overnight."

Tomas looked at Lei Chen. "I'm going to assume the Professor won't expect me to be behind him because he thinks I'm paralyzed. I have some tracking skills, but I can't guarantee that he won't discover that I'm following him."

"Hannah and Tamlyn will be on the trail, drawing him forward. He might look for you as he climbs upward. Just stay out of sight as much as possible. Remember: No phone calls. Olivia and David will monitor from the air with the drones. Text me when you are nearing the cave," Lei Chen requested.

"I want to know where Gustav is at all times," Hannah whispered. "I'm texting Olivia to give us updates on his path. Do you think he will stay out overnight?"

Tomas shrugged his shoulders. "We need to sleep, but maybe we can rotate the night watch on Gustav."

"Four-hour shifts should work well. We'd better get going. At this rate, we won't reach the cave until after sundown." Lei Chen motioned them to start upward.

Tamlyn and Tomas shook their heads. This was the hard part, knowingly going into danger.

As they hiked, Tamlyn slowed her normal stride to match the pace of Hannah and Lei Chen. As they moved up the trail, she felt the urge to grow darker, to walk closer to the shaded pines.

Hannah noticed Tamlyn edging toward the trees and put her arm around her shoulders. "I know that this is frightening for you. If you feel threatened, do what you must to protect yourself," Hannah told her.

"I feel safer closer to the trees. I can blend into the shadows easily there," Tamlyn said.

"We can all walk closer to the tree line," Lei Chen said.

"I hope you don't mind, but I'd rather go ahead of you," Tamlyn explained. "My nervous energy can get me to the cave quickly, where I can rest and wait for you."

Hannah cocked her head at Lei Chen. "What do you think?"

"I'd rather keep together, but she has a point," Lei Chen said. "It would be safer to keep us between her and Gustav. Tamlyn, go ahead, but text us every thirty to forty-five minutes. It shouldn't take you more than three hours to get to the cave. At our pace, we will be an hour behind you."

A few minutes later, Tomas texted Lei Chen:

Gustav hasn't come out of the cabin yet. I think I should start up toward the cave. I'll keep watching for him, but I'm going to stay off the path. If things change, I'll let you know.

Chapter 32: Confrontation on the Bridge

During the night in the cave, Hannah asked Tomas to try putting the pieces together, hoping he could get a glimpse of what would happen the next day.

Tomas sat back and closed his eyes. His hands started to tremble as sweat dripped from his forehead.

"I see flashes of Tamlyn and the Professor on the Bridge to Forever. The Professor is trying to give a cup of something to Tamlyn to drink—then it fades to darkness. I see the Professor falling onto the bridge. Now I see Lei Chen with a black box in his hands. Tamlyn is running away. There is movement from other people, but I can't see them clearly." Tomas stopped, taking a few deep breaths.

"I don't know who they are or why they are there," he continued. "Maybe it's the team from the other side of the bridge."

Tomas opened his eyes and shook his head as if trying to clear the visions.

"What I saw is the most likely scenario. But I think Gustav is bound to have a secondary plan, and we don't know anything about that. It could be a weapon, something only he can control."

Hannah turned toward Tamlyn and saw that she was very pale. "Listen to me, young lady. If we see Gustav trying to give you something, I'll call out to him and try to get him to turn around to face me. I know this isn't part of the plan, but based on what Tomas is seeing, I think we might need a distraction to keep you safe."

"Don't worry, Hannah. Mr. Suweto was very thorough in teaching me techniques to keep Professor von Telleman from touching me. I practice them every time I close my eyes. I'm ready." She gave Hannah a brief smile.

"I'll take the first watch," Hannah told the group. "Get some sleep now. I'll wake Lei Chen next for his watch."

The next morning just after sunrise, Lei Chen, groggy and sore from the climb and lack of sleep, prompted the rest of the team to get moving and continue with their plan. Gustav was a no-show, which sent Tomas back down the mountain path to the cabin. Tamlyn, Hannah, and Lei Chen continued up the mountain toward their next checkpoint.

After forty minutes of hard climbing, Lei Chen was winded, so he decided to check in with the Eastside team's progress. Teani reported that after breakfast, the boys had left to check on the goat. He had eaten some of the vegetation they left for him and was resting comfortably. She said that they continued up to the bridge. Logan would reach it first, maybe as early as 2 p.m., and she thought the boys would reach the bridge shortly before dusk.

Lei Chen texted Teani that Tomas was watching for Gustav and would follow him, giving them updates of his position on the mountain. The Westside team would come together again in a cave closer to the bridge before interacting with Gustav.

✦ ✦ ✦

Gustav launched his drone to watch Tamlyn and the rest of the team during their hike up the mountain. *Surprise! Look who has joined the team. Hannah, you have neither the stamina nor strength to keep up with me. You can't protect Tamlyn, and I will deal with you if you get in my way. You have no idea about the metal-dissolving chemicals I planted under the west side of the bridge two nights ago. It was so stupid of you to post so many details about the Challenge for the teachers.*

Gustav thought that Tomas and Tamlyn would share the water from his canteen. But he realized that Tomas was not following the same path as the rest of the group. *Where is he? I should have set up some traps along the path, but I had to stay out of sight once they knew I was here. I'll prepare another thermos with the paralyzing solution. Both Hannah and Tamlyn will be thirsty by the time they reach the bridge.*

Gustav believed that Lei Chen would not be a problem. He was an administrator, a paper pusher—not an obstacle. Gustav secured the newly filled thermos to the outside of his pack that contained climbing rope, pitons, his own canteen, a flashlight, and the detonation device. With everything packed, he closed the blinds, locked the front door of the cabin, and started up the mountain.

✦ ✦ ✦

Tomas watched Gustav, staying back until he was sure that Gustav wouldn't see or hear him trailing behind. He texted an update to Lei Chen and kept pace with Gustav. Gustav's legs were long and strong. He looked like mountain climbing was his favorite hobby, maintaining a brisk pace. About halfway up the mountain, Gustav stopped, removed a canteen from his pack, and took several large gulps before returning it to the pack.

Tomas wondered why he wasn't drinking from the thermos, which he could see was more easily accessible. But based on his visions from the night in the cave, Tomas realized that the liquid in the thermos was probably the solution Gustav had boiled in the pot at the back of the cabin. He sent a quick text about the thermos to Lei Chen.

The return text said:

> It probably contains the same solution he put in your canteen. No results yet from the Queenstown analysis. We'll assume it's toxic. Keep up, but stay out of sight. Let us know when he's getting close to us.

Tamlyn worked her way up the mountain with Lei Chen and Hannah trailing behind her. They were both winded and sweating. "Let's stop for a minute. You need to drink some water and rest. What's going on?" Tamlyn asked Lei Chen.

"Tomas is behind Professor von Telleman," he said, drying his face with a small towel he pulled from his pack. "He has both a thermos and a canteen and is climbing up toward the bridge. He's not drinking from the thermos, so we can draw our own conclusions from that. Tomas says he's past the halfway point, so we better get going. When we get to the checkpoint, we'll review the next steps of the plan." Lei Chen motioned for Tamlyn to go ahead of him and slowly returned to the climb.

A short while later, Tamlyn stopped, hid behind a large boulder, then turned to look down the mountain. She caught sight of Gustav and waited until Lei Chen caught up to her. "My instinct to camouflage is starting. I feel more afraid as we get closer to the bridge. As long as we are in the forest, my ability to blend in will protect me. But Hannah, how will you protect yourself if he decides to vent his anger on you?" Tamlyn asked as she faded into the shadows between the trees.

"All of us are prepared to fight back," Hannah said. "You just need to concentrate on climbing quietly now that you are hidden. Gustav is a woodsman, and he will rely on all his senses to find you. I'm just a distraction. Tomas will be helping as well. And the other team will meet us on the opposite side of the bridge. Go now."

Tamlyn's heart pounded, and her legs ached from the steep climb. *I've got to make it,* she told herself. *Professor von Telleman has got to be stopped. All I have to do is follow the plan.*

When Tamlyn reached the cave that was the next checkpoint later in the afternoon, she was nearly spent. She drank the spring water from her canteen and wolfed down a travel bar of nuts, raisins, seeds, and honey. She felt better after a few minutes and watched for the rest of the group. Tamlyn knew that she would need to reappear to draw Gustav in. She didn't know if she could control her talent that way when danger was near. Her camouflage was fading as she rested, but she remained partially hidden.

About fifteen minutes later, Hannah crept quietly into the cave. "Tamlyn, is that you?" she asked.

"Yes. Are you okay, Hannah?" Tamlyn replied.

"I'm in no shape for mountain climbing, that's for sure." Hannah drank from her canteen and continued. "Gustav's not on the path now. He headed off into the trees, and we lost sight of him."

Lei Chen was perspiring heavily as he entered the cave. He pulled a scarf from around his neck to wipe his face and glasses. "Whew! I didn't think we would have to climb this mountain so quickly. I'm more out of shape than I thought. How are you feeling, Tamlyn? I can see parts of you on and off."

"I was really tired when I got here, but I am better now. Did you see Tomas anywhere?" she asked anxiously.

"He is trailing the Professor and went off into the trees. He might have to wait for the Professor to get above us. Then he'll check in. The sun is moving behind the mountain, and dusk will quickly follow. Tomas will stay close to you. Hannah and I will stay in the trees on the west side of the bridge. If it would make you feel better, we could tie a rope around you, and then we could use that to pull you away from him if needed," he said.

Tamlyn shook her head. "No, the rope can't be camouflaged. He will detect it and know exactly where I am." She breathed deeply and saw the rest of the trail clearly in her mind. She knew she could get to the bridge without help from the rest of the team. It was important for her to get there first so that Professor von Telleman would approach her. She regretted that she had never known her half-brother when she was growing up. Her hopes that he might abandon his plans and become a better person were fading away.

Tomas texted some new information:

Gustav launched a drone before he left the cabin. I don't know if he is controlling it or if it is following a programmed flight plan, but it is moving toward the bridge.

"Does everyone know what to do now?" Lei Chen asked.

Tamlyn said, "I'll hike up to the bridge, making myself darker all the way. I will walk out onto the bridge, then slowly start to show myself. Professor von Telleman should come out to talk with me. I'll keep my distance from him but engage him in conversation. If he tries to hand me a cup, Hannah will call out to distract him."

Lei Chen said, "I'm glad Tomas reminded me about the box; I almost forgot about it. No matter what happens, I will keep it ready. I don't have time to explain what it does. The other team should be very close to the bridge by now. We don't want them to run into Professor von Telleman."

Then Lei Chen texted Teani to warn the team about the confrontation that would shortly take place on the bridge.

> **Don't use flashlights. It might cause the danger to spread to your group. Tell Nick to be ready if we must get physical to stop Gustav. Hahona, Logan, and Enrique should be ready to help Tamlyn.**

"Tamlyn, are you ready?" Lei Chen asked.

Tamlyn nodded and stepped out of the cave. In the hazy dusk, it was easy for her to fade from sight. She saw Gustav at the west end of the bridge. He had a flashlight and was scanning around the area. The light did not reach the east end of the bridge, where the other team was waiting. Tamlyn walked past Gustav toward the center of the bridge, just past the place where his flashlight stopped. She saw Tomas and Hannah creeping up behind Gustav. Then she turned toward him and called, "Hello, Professor von Telleman. I see you are out hiking, too. Isn't it beautiful up here?" Her voice shook with tension.

Gustav stepped onto the bridge and flashed the light toward Tamlyn's voice. "Who is there? I can't see you."

Slowly, Tamlyn began to appear against the background of the bridge. She took a small step forward toward the flashlight beam. "You know me. I'm Tamlyn Reiter," she said softly.

"Tamlyn! I thought I saw you hiking this way earlier. I love climbing in the mountains. It is good exercise and full of new things to see," he said.

Tamlyn tried to see Gustav's face. He sounded so friendly and calm. But it was too dark. He was just a darker patch in the spreading gloom.

"It was a difficult hike, and I am tired. But you're right. It is worth the effort," she replied.

"So, you climbed up here by yourself?" Gustav asked.

Tamlyn nodded but kept her distance. She could see Tomas and Hannah crawling onto the bridge. They moved slowly to keep the noise to a minimum. Water falling from the mountain into the stream below the bridge helped to mask the sound of their movements.

Gustav slowly approached the center of the bridge. He didn't want to scare Tamlyn into running from him. "I brought some water with me. I imagine you are thirsty," he said, walking toward her with the thermos in his hand.

"That's okay, Professor. I have my own canteen with water."

Gustav took a few more steps toward her, scanning the bridge with his flashlight, wondering, *Where is the rest of her team?* He knew they would be somewhere nearby. He must get to Tamlyn before they could arrive and interfere.

"I make a special water with electrolytes in it to replenish expended energy after such a long climb," he explained.

Tamlyn knew this was the time to fully show herself. She felt her skin cooling in the night air, and then the beam from Gustav's flashlight illuminated her face.

Gustav walked toward her more quickly now. "Ah, there you are. Here," he said, holding out the thermos cup with the paralyzing liquid. "Drink some of this, and you will feel much better." Gustav grabbed her hand, but Tamlyn quickly pressed hard against his wrist tendons, forcing him to release her.

Hannah watched Tamlyn free herself from Gustav's grasp. *Great job, Tamlyn! Now it's our turn.*

Tomas and Hannah launched themselves against Gustav's legs. As he fell backward, the water in the cup splashed into Gustav's face and mouth. He screamed as he fell onto the bridge. Tamlyn thought she heard a crunch as his shoulder hit the metal slats. Tomas pushed Gustav against the railing and motioned for Tamlyn to go. But she was frozen in place, watching Professor von Telleman's face as he realized what had happened.

Chapter 33: The Final Act

Gustav pushed himself onto his knees with one arm, grimacing in pain. He stared up at Tamlyn and snarled, "You think you are soooo spesshalll, inheriting our mother's giffftt of fading away. Growing up in Aussstria with herrr." His words became slower and slurred as he spoke. "Well, you willlll not essscape yurrr fate," he growled.

Tomas tried to hold Gustav still, but his hands were becoming numb where the liquid from the thermos had splashed him. Gustav wrenched his body away from Tomas to reach into his pack. He fumbled for a minute, then pushed the bag over. The detonation device to trigger the metal-dissolving chemicals fell out. Gustav threw his arm over the buttons to activate it. Tomas backed away from him, thinking that he had an explosive weapon that could kill them all. As Gustav lay still against the bottom of the guard rail, smoke began to billow up from under the bridge. But there were no explosions, only the scream of metal ripping apart.

Lei Chen was running to help Tomas. He activated the SonoPrep as soon as he reached him, pulling him back toward the forest path and safety.

On the east side of the bridge, Nick pulled Hahona up to the crossing. "We need to get out there and help the other team. Are you ready?" Nick asked.

Hahona nodded and reached for Nick's hand.

Tamlyn felt someone grab her arm and pull her away from Gustav. Hannah held one arm and Hahona held the other.

"Come with us right now," Hannah said. "Nick, go help Tomas and Lei Chen. Hurry! The bridge is about to collapse. We'll meet you back at the project." Looking into Tamlyn's shocked face, Hannah started to pull her arm. "If we run, we can reach the east side! Come on!"

Tamlyn ran with them as fast as she could. It was too dark to see anything. Before she reached the eastern edge, she looked behind her and could see a body falling from the bridge into the ravine.

"Tomas!" Tamlyn screamed. "Are you okay?"

"Yes! Get off the bridge!" he yelled back. "Don't stop!"

The Bridge to Forever collapsed, raining planks, dissolving metal wires, and ropes down into the chasm. Gustav and his paralytic solution, the detonator, and pack disappeared into the dark.

Tamlyn, Hannah, and Hahona safely reached the east side of the ravine as the smoke cleared and the melting metal fell into the chasm below. Teani pulled Tamlyn toward her. "Are you hurt? Let me look at you," she said. "Enrique, hold the flashlight on her."

Tamlyn realized she must be suffering from shock. Voices were muffled. The light in her face kept her from seeing the people around her. But she felt Hannah's arms around her, holding her as Teani did a head-to-toe check.

Time to call Lei Chen. "Hi, it's Teani. Tamlyn, Hannah, and my team are safe on the east side of the ravine. I can't find any injuries on Tamlyn or Hannah, but we should get them to medical to be checked. How is Tomas? Is Nick with you?" she asked.

"I don't have time to talk to you now. I'm treating Tomas, and Nick is here helping me. As soon as everyone is calm, start heading back to the project. Make sure to tell the children how proud we are of them," Lei Chen instructed.

"Of course. Take your time. And you should congratulate the team there as well. You did quite well—for a paper pusher!" She laughed in relief and signed off.

✦✦✦

Hahona wrapped a blanket around Tamlyn, who was visibly shaking. "Thank you for following and trusting me. Do you need to rest?" he asked.

Tamlyn didn't know how to respond to that question. She tried to calm down by telling herself, *The danger has passed. You are with friends. Take deep breaths.*

Hahona watched as she worked to gain control. "We will be heading back to the project site in a little while. With the bridge gone, the other team will have to go back on the southwest path. It sounds like they are okay, but that path is steeper, and they will have to go more slowly."

When she could finally see everyone around her, Tamlyn realized that it was Professor von Telleman's body that had fallen into the ravine. She saw the image vividly in her mind and realized that it so easily could have been her or Tomas or Hannah. *That's why I'm trembling. It's time to walk down the mountain. You can do this if you keep your emotions in check. Don't burden the rest of the group with taking care of you.*

Logan and Enrique had already gathered their supplies and started down the eastside path. Then Teani motioned to the rest of the group to start walking down the path toward the dark forest. Tamlyn tried to talk to Hahona but couldn't get the words out.

Tamlyn knew she could have been splashed with the toxin and become paralyzed. From the look of worry on Hannah's face, it was clear she had the same thought. Tamlyn took a deep breath and cleared her throat, trying to talk. "I can walk. Hahona, will you help me?" she whispered. *I don't know much about him, but he seems like a very compassionate child.* Concentrating on him and the path would keep her mind engaged.

As they began walking, Hannah realized that her left knee hurt. She reached down to feel it—no blood, but it was swollen. She watched as Hahona took charge of caring for Tamlyn. He seemed to instinctively know what she needed, so Hannah walked behind them, keeping her flashlight on the path at their feet.

Hahona held Tamlyn's hand as they walked, telling her about his family and growing up in New Zealand. Despite her fatigue, shock, and disorientation, Tamlyn found herself calming down as he told his story. She could almost see him roaming the meadows for medicinal plants, learning from the elders of his tribe, swimming in the ocean and lakes, and watching as the animals lived and worked in their natural habitats. He told her about the first time he saw someone die. He said that the elder simply decided it was time. Hahona wasn't ready for that. The emptiness filled his chest, and he told her his thought: *This is grief.*

Tamlyn thought she understood Hahona's gift—learning what it takes to nurture people, animals, and plants so that all thrived together. He was another child with amazing gifts, who did not hesitate to reach out to help her when she was in trouble. She had done her part to counteract the danger, and so had he. She began to feel that the project was *her* tribal community now. *It is where I belong.*

Teani watched Logan in the lead and moved back to talk with Hannah. She described how Enrique and Hahona worked together to take care of the injured goat. They used their skills and knowledge to create a plan, not hesitating to carry it out. Hannah felt the strength of the people around her, taking comfort in their presence.

Hours later, as dawn was just peeking out from the mountaintops, Teani's team arrived safely back at the project site. Teani and Hahona took Tamlyn to the medical facility, briefly relating the shocking events on the bridge. Before the doctors could take Tamlyn to an exam room, she said, "Wait." Then she turned to Hahona and smiled through her tears. "Thank you for taking care of me and for showing me your life. I hope that we can be friends."

Hahona gave her a brief bow. "I honor you for your courage. We are already friends. We have shared an adventure that we will always remember. I look forward to completing other Challenges with you."

Tamlyn wiped the tears from her face and waved goodbye as the doctors took her to the exam room. They drew blood, gave her a mild antibiotic, checked her blood pressure and physical reflexes, and then put her to bed under a warmed blanket.

Teani waited in the room until Tamlyn was asleep, and then she sought out Lei Chen.

He told her that he had been with Tomas, using the SonoPrep device that Hannah had given him to remove the toxins from Tomas's hands. Nick washed Tomas down with water from his canteen after the device had been activated for twenty minutes. Tomas showed no signs of further paralysis, and when he had warmed up, they started hiking back.

Lei Chen went to Tamlyn's room with the SonoPrep device. If there was any of the paralyzing agent in her, the device would allow it to exit her pores harmlessly while she slept. Teani described how well Tamlyn did on the return trip. She said that although Tamlyn was obviously tired and stressed from the traumatic encounter, she remained alert, walking normally and talking with Hahona. Lei Chen heaved a sigh of relief, leaving the device with the medical staff.

$$\star\;\star\;\star$$

Although the adults were tired, Hannah knew it was time to let Sarah Dowie and her law enforcement contacts know that a death had occurred. Sitting with an ice pack on her knee, Hannah called Sarah from the Medical Center.

"Hello, Hannah." Sarah's voice was soft as she answered the phone. "Have there been any new developments?" she asked.

"Where to begin?" Hannah's voice was shaky, but there was no putting this off. "Professor Gustav von Telleman tried to get members of the project to drink a paralyzing solution he created during their Challenge exercise on the mountain. He particularly targeted a young woman named Tamlyn Reiter. During a confrontation on the bridge spanning a large ravine, he triggered the release of a chemical that he had planted under it that dissolved the metal support structures. He fell to his death last night."

Sarah was silent for several moments. "So that was the danger your special children were feeling. I expect that you need my law enforcement contacts now. However, before I give you their names, please tell me whether anyone else was harmed."

Hannah stuttered. "I ... I ... really don't think I can tell you more without breaking down. I'm trying to do what I can to keep this under wraps until the investigators arrive. We will guide them along the mountain and bridge areas, including the cabin Gustav was using." She blew her nose at that point, then took some deep breaths.

"Listen, I won't press you for more now," Sarah said. "I will text you the names and phone numbers of the New Zealand Police officers in your area, after I brief them. You can call them when you are ready. Keep everyone out of the mountain areas that are part of the investigation," Sarah cautioned.

"Thank you, Sarah." Hannah's thoughts were spinning. *How will XL-ENCE survive this disaster?*

Hannah texted Stephen, asking him to contact Dirk Jackson to let him know what happened. Later in the day, the project site was buzzing with the events that had happened at the Bridge to Forever. Hannah called Olivia and requested a video meeting. Olivia activated the meeting site and invited Hannah in.

"I don't have much to report right now," Olivia explained. "Lei Chen and Teani are sleeping. Like you, Tamlyn and Tomas are at the Medical Center. They woke up a little while ago. The staff says they will do more tests later, but their initial blood tests were normal. Tamlyn asked for Amanda, and they have been talking for about twenty minutes now."

"I'll call her as soon as we're finished. How much was captured on the drones?" Hannah asked.

"You can see for yourself. After darkness fell, the transmission was not good enough to see what was going on. You should check in with Maya and James to get more details about how we are handling this." Olivia started to yawn. "I'm pooped! You know, I didn't sign up for this! After I restrict viewing of the drone footage on the website, I'm going to sleep for at least ten hours!"

"Well done, Olivia. Sleep tight!"

Hannah called Amanda next. "How is Tamlyn doing? Are you still with her? Please tell me as much as you can."

Amanda stepped out of the room to talk with Hannah. "She looks good. We have been talking about her family. I think Tamlyn needs to see her mum. She had a lot of questions about her half-brother that only her mum could answer. Is it possible for us to fly her in?"

"Of course. We'll get started on that right away. Amanda, please stay with her for as long as she needs you," Hannah requested.

"I'll stay for a while, and then I'll switch off with Teani or Tomas. I think she asked for me because I met her family when we recruited her."

"Tamlyn knows what she needs now. The local New Zealand Police officers will be coming to the project site tomorrow. They will want to talk with her before they start investigating the mountain. Let her know this is coming. Call or text me if you need anything else."

✦✦✦

The next day, Olivia and Nick were the first members of the Management Team to meet the Police— two officers, the coroner, and three detectives assigned under the command of Senior Sergeant Beckford. Nick explained the steps they had taken prior to initiating the climb up the mountain. Olivia showed them the drone footage and Gustav von Telleman's application and personnel file and the results of her patent search. Nick also gave the officers the contacts from the construction crew who had personally interacted with Gustav.

The officers interviewed Tamlyn, Tomas, Lei Chen, and Hannah regarding the events on the mountain. The chemical analysis from Queenstown had been received that morning, and the report was given to the officers as part of the evidence along with the sample containers.

Hannah called Logan and M'gera asking them to meet her at the cabin. She was bringing the detectives with her to review the evidence. She asked Logan to show them Gustav's laptop with the footage from his drone along with the letter from Gustav's mother and his lab. M'gera would escort them along the path to the remains of the bridge. Then she would take them back along the path to the bottom of the chasm, where Gustav's mangled body, thermos, pack, and the detonator were located.

It took nearly seven hours to compile the information and review it with the detectives to make sure nothing was left out. They all reached one inescapable conclusion: Gustav had intended to kill Tamlyn.

While Logan, M'gera, and Hannah remained in the cabin, Senior Sergeant Beckford collected the physical evidence and placed it into the back of his jeep. The coroner and officers retrieved Gustav's body from the chasm, loading it into the police van.

"We will follow up with you in a few days," the Sergeant told Hannah.

After the law enforcement officers were finished gathering the evidence, Hannah was faced with another problem: how to convince the lawyers Gustav's actions and death were not a failure of the XL-ENCE project. What would the students, their families, and the surrounding community do when they found out one of the teachers was a killer?

Logan could feel how upset Hannah was becoming. It was starting to rain, so he motioned for M'gera to join him in the kitchen while he made tea for them.

"Hannah really needs our support now," he told her. "I'd like to stay here with her. What do you think we should do now? I would appreciate your input."

Working with M'gera was humbling for him. She did the most extraordinary things and made them look so easy.

M'gera looked at Logan and grinned. He used to act superior to the other Accelerators at the beginning. Now, thanks to James and Amanda, he understood how their skills could be combined to make things better and that everyone was of equal value to the project. "If it was me, I would take a long walk in the rain to get re-centered," M'gera said. "But I think Hannah should talk to Hahona and Adisa. This project is Hannah's vision for a better world. And the more we work with her to make it come alive, the better she will feel. I'm going to head back to the children's dormitory. I'll call you when Hahona and Adisa can talk." She pulled out her rain gear and headed out the back door.

Logan brought the tea into the front room and sat at the table across from Hannah. "Here, drink this," he said. "M'gera has gone back to the children's dormitory."

Hannah took the cup, holding it and staring out at the rain. The two sat silently for over an hour, lost in their thoughts.

Finally, Logan said, "Will you talk to me about why you are so worried?"

Hannah struggled to bring her thoughts back to the present. She could see that Logan was genuinely concerned for her. His green eyes were so compassionate. "Thank you for your concern," Hannah said. "This project means so much to me. I'm afraid this incident will be the end for us. In my heart, I know justice was served, and we did everything we could. But we haven't had much time to develop community support. I think this will scare them. What can I say?" A tear rolled down her cheek as she tried to smile.

Logan touched her hand as he handed her a napkin for her tears. "Hannah, I can't predict the future. But we have so many good people here. The things we can accomplish, that no one else can, are too important to stop. I think other people feel that way, too."

"I hope you're right, Logan," Hannah said.

At that moment, M'gera notified Logan that the children were ready to talk with Hannah.

"Hannah, M'gera wants us to hear what Hahona and Adisa have to say. Are you ready?" Hannah nodded. Hahona appeared on the screen, looking calm and older than his ten years.

"You were right about the bridge, Hahona," Hannah told him. "I want to thank you for your bravery and the help you gave me and Tamlyn when we were in danger. I hope you enjoyed the rest of the Challenge. It was supposed to be a learning experience, not life or death."

"No matter what tribe you are in, we must take care of each other," Hahona said. He hesitated for a few moments, then smiled at Hannah. "This project is like the strong, beating heart in a new baby that needs to be taught and nurtured."

Hannah was surprised at that analogy. What an interesting way to see the world! She was comforted and not surprised when Adisa took his place on the screen.

"Hello, Miss Hannah," she said. "Don't be sad. Ask me the question that is in your heart, and I will tell you what I see."

"Oh, Adisa, will the project be able to continue?" Hannah whispered. She was almost too afraid to ask.

Adisa closed her eyes. "Nona would say, *'If you believe.'* As Hahona said, 'The new baby is strong.' We want to see it grow up. Don't be afraid. We won't leave you alone." She opened her eyes and said, "Come back."

M'gera pulled Adisa away and sent her off to dinner with Hahona. "Yes, Adisa is right. Both of you, come back. The rain is light, and you should be able to get here before the trails get too slippery."

"Thank you, M'gera. We will clean up here and start back as soon as we can," Hannah said.

Chapter 34: The Future of the Project

When Hannah returned to her office, she briefed Nick and Stephen about the New Zealand Senior Sergeant's conclusions. Sister Angelique and Father Brennan offered to drive in to provide counseling and support for the children and their families. They thought that the entire project staff, students, and families deserved to know the truth about what had happened in the forest. It would serve as a reminder that there was still evil in the world as well as wonderful new things to learn and try. Lei Chen and Olivia had discussed this approach with the Accelerators, who agreed that knowing the truth would be the best for everyone.

Tamlyn's mother, Viktoria, arrived at the Queenstown airport at noon, three days after law enforcement had completed their investigation. Amanda was there to meet her. She had insisted that Tamlyn stay at the project with Teani or Lei Chen. After they retrieved Viktoria's luggage, Amanda started to tell her about Gustav.

"Viktoria, you knew that Tamlyn joined our project because of the unique ability you and Tamlyn share. What you didn't know was that your son, Gustav, was hired here as a chemistry teacher." Amanda was driving and couldn't risk looking at Viktoria's face. "We didn't know that they were related. We think Gustav discovered their relationship first. He ... was bloody upset about it. In fact, he wanted to hurt her the way that his father had hurt him."

"Oh no!" Viktoria gasped. "Is Tamlyn all right?"

"Yes, but wait, there is more, and it's pretty ugly. He developed a plan to kill her, and during the attempt, he destroyed the bridge they were standing on and fell to his death."

Viktoria exhaled sharply. "I should never have left him with that bastard! Oh, Gustav! What did I do to you?" When Viktoria started to cry, Amanda pulled the car to the side of the road and stopped, waiting until Tamlyn's mother was calmer.

"I'm sorry for your loss," Amanda said. "But Tamlyn needs you very badly. You don't have to talk much, but it will help her to know that you're here. Do you think you are ready to see her? She feels the loss of a brother she never had. Has she ever experienced someone dying before?"

Viktoria took a handkerchief out of her purse and blew her nose loudly. "No. This is her first experience with a person's death. I should have told her about Gustav, but I was so afraid that Heinrich would find us. I am such a coward."

"We can't do anything about the past. It's the actions we take now that are important." Amanda started the car and pulled back onto the road. The project site was only about fifteen minutes away.

"I will grieve for Gustav later." Viktoria turned to Amanda and looked into her eyes. "Thank you for taking care of Tamlyn. I am ready to see her."

When they arrived at the recovery section of the medical building, Tamlyn jumped out of her bed and yelled, "Mama!" She and Viktoria stood holding each other for what seemed like a long time to Amanda. She wanted to let Tamlyn take control of the meeting with her mother. So Amanda waited outside of the room as they began to talk.

✦ ✦ ✦

Two days later, Sister Angelique and Father Brennan requested a meeting with Nick, Maya, and James to discuss the children and their families. Maya took the lead as the official liaison between the project and the Queenstown community.

"First of all, we appreciate the support you've provided to the children and their families in the wake of Professor von Telleman's death. We've provided you with the evidence collected from the cabin Gustav was using and the materials collected after the destruction of the bridge. Why have you requested this meeting?" she asked.

"There was no way to keep the information from spreading to the community in Queenstown, especially after law enforcement became involved. We provided the facts but left the people alone to reach their own conclusions. Two families from our church wanted to reach out to help the children," Father Brennan explained.

Sister Angelique continued. "They want to take them to the Orana Wildlife Park in Christchurch. They feel terrible about what happened to a project that is dedicated to helping people find a better way to live together. They asked if the project could provide vans or buses for the drive. Everyone could see something of New Zealand, a new country to most of them, during the trip. The Wildlife Park would be a great place for them to relax and learn about the native animals. They could even stay overnight in Christchurch."

Maya was stunned. *What a compassionate and thoughtful idea.*

James jumped at the chance to build more community support. Back in New Zealand for consultation with law enforcement, Stephen also thought the trip was a great idea and gave them financial approval for anything they needed, handing two credit cards to James. It was a wild scramble, getting the children ready for the trip. Everyone filled overnight backpacks with pajamas and other essentials. The commissary made bag lunches for them, with extra snacks for the drive. Three vans were ready to go by 10 a.m. Other families from the community joined the caravan, bringing their own children. Families of the children in the project were invited on the trip by Father Brennan, who loaded them into the church van and utility vehicles.

Hannah and Nick stayed behind, waving goodbye to the children and reminding them to text pictures of the Wildlife Park back to the staff. They wanted to work with Lei Chen, Teani, and the Accelerators to see what was happening with them. Caught in the middle of recent events, they had performed beyond expectations. But no one on the Management Team knew what they were feeling.

Hannah feared the worst. "Nick, I'm sure some of them will want to leave the project. They didn't sign up for this kind of danger."

"Hold on, Hannah. Give them a chance! This isn't an academic project. I think they understood the risks when they signed those contracts. Let's go see what Lei Chen and Teani are doing with them." He took her hand and led her to the main conference room in the Administration building.

Everyone wanted to be there to exchange ideas about what had happened. The room was crowded and noisy. Teani clapped her hands for quiet.

"Thank you for coming. As an empath, I am being overwhelmed by the strong emotions you are feeling. If we are going to move forward, I need you to calm yourselves for a few moments. Just take some deep breaths and exhale slowly." A short while later, she resumed speaking. "Hannah and Nick are here from the Management Team to hear your concerns. I have spoken to most of you regarding the events at the bridge and the evidence that was found afterward. Tell us what you would like to do and how you feel. Almost all of you were involved in one way or another. Who would like to start?"

Amanda raised her hand. Teani nodded for her to begin. "As the danger from Professor von Telleman became more apparent, I was worried about whether we would be able to stop him. However, everyone was so open about it. The children talked to each other and to us. The Management Team involved us in their plans. We had important responsibilities. The Accelerators never said no, no matter what was asked of them. The hardest thing I had to do was tell Tamlyn's mother about Professor von Telleman's death. She didn't know he was here, and that Tamlyn was in danger from him. She was a real trooper—pulled herself together and wanted to help. There is that feeling here—pulling together and wanting to help. That's why I'm staying."

Hannah's eyebrows crept toward her hairline. Amanda's story was so unexpected.

Teani asked, "Who wants to go next?"

Tomas stood up. "It's hard to describe what I experienced. I never felt like I was alone, even when I was tracking Professor von Telleman by myself through the forest. He had so many chances to be a better person. Tamlyn wanted him to be the brother she never had. That's why she volunteered to draw him out. My part seemed so small compared to what she was doing. This project means something different to each of us. For me, I have a new family here. I want to share the hard work, the learning that comes from failure, the joy that comes from success."

Teani felt the Accelerators coming together. Not one of them wanted to leave. But they had some important issues to deal with now.

"I am opening this meeting for ideas. As with all brainstorming sessions, all ideas are welcome. There are pads of paper on easels around the room for us to write our ideas on. But the main topic is this: *Danger Training.* We first need to identify dangerous situations, for example, forest fires. The pads on the east side of the room are for Danger Situations. The pads on the west side of the room are for Training Ideas for the children. We also need to prepare ourselves to handle danger. The pads on the south side of the room are for ideas for Accelerator training. The pads on the north side are for Hannah and Nick to use for the Management Team." Teani paused as the Accelerators looked around the room.

"Before you write down your ideas, please check the pads to see if the idea has already been suggested. You can move around the room to the different areas to think about what's there. I ask that you speak softly, in consideration of others. We have the conference room booked for the rest of the day. I will upload all suggestions to our Accelerator file on the website. Tomorrow, we can review the suggestions and do some prioritizing. But I would like to have something ready for Management Team review soon. They will be meeting with the lawyers handling the project funds for our benefactor, Robert Langer, next week. Are there any questions?"

Logan raised his hand. Teani nodded at him to speak. "It's likely that the community nearby has plans and training for fighting fires. We could ask them to share the plans with us and maybe do some training. That will show them that we respect the land and want to work with them."

"A very good suggestion. Please write it down on the pad for Accelerator Training. Anyone else?" Teani asked. When no other hands were raised, she said, "Let's go."

✦✦✦

Later that day, photos from the Wildlife Park came pouring in from the children and their families.

Children from Queenstown and the project gathered around kiwis, kakapo birds, geckos, and penguins. There were lots of smiles and sunburnt noses. One picture showed Hahona licking Manuka honey off his fingers. James and Maya sent multiple messages about the adults:

You should see Father Brennan with Nona. They have become the unofficial Park guides for our group. Sister Angelique fell in love with the orchid gardens. She happily led others through the trees to see the many species of orchid that are native to New Zealand.

Many of the people from Queenstown had never been to the Wildlife Park. The sea lions bark, making lots of raucous noise, causing everyone to laugh. And, of course, they are stuffing us with lamb dishes and pavlova! We couldn't have asked for a nicer field trip. Hope everything is going well there.

That evening, Nick called Hannah. "If you can spare some time for me, I have something special that I'd like to give you. Please come over whenever you can. I'll be waiting." He hung up, leaving Hannah wondering.

Her heart started pounding. Alone time with Nick! She had so much to say to him. If Maya was her right arm, Nick was her left. It was late when Hannah knocked on Nick's door. She felt guilty when he called out, "Just a minute. I'll be right there."

He opened the door in his pajama bottoms, toweling his hair dry. She was again struck by how tall and slim he was. He exuded an aura of strength that made him seem larger than life. She stood in the doorway, admiring the view.

"If you need a formal invitation, I'll have to get my tux from the cleaners," he teased.

Hannah blushed and pushed him aside as she came in. "I'm sorry I'm so late. There never seems to be enough hours in the day."

"Tea?" Nick asked, pulling her into the living room by the fireplace.

"No, I just want to talk now," she replied.

"Let me put this towel away and put on a shirt. I'll be right back."

When Nick returned, he sat next to Hannah, inhaling the fragrance of her hair that reminded him of the flowers that grew around his house when he was a boy. "You have my undivided attention."

"Nick, I don't know what will happen when we meet with the attorneys, and I wish that we didn't have to face this crisis so soon. But I worry about how this will affect you. You gave up a lot to join this project. You mean so much to me, and I will do whatever it takes to make sure you have excellent references for any future career you want."

Nick looked into her big grey-blue eyes and gently kissed her. "You can't get rid of me that easily. There is a tradition in the Ukraine that has been kept in my family for many generations." He opened the middle drawer in the coffee table and took out a small box. "This is a Promise ring. It was my mother's, and her mother's, and it might have been worn by many others. It is my promise to always be at your side whenever you need me. It is my promise to always give you my best. And it is my promise to keep you in my heart until I am no more than dust."

The ring was a small band of white gold with a heart-shaped ruby and a small, round diamond next to it. Hannah's hand trembled as she reached for the ring. "Really? This is for me? It is so beautiful."

Nick placed the ring on the third finger of Hannah's right hand. "You're stuck with me now, bright eyes."

"Oh, Nick. This is one of the happiest moments of my life. I will never forget it."

"Neither will I. Time to sleep now," Nick said as he banked the fire.

Chapter 35: The Lawyers

Now Hannah's only worry was the lawyers. Although Stephen had contacted them the morning after the Challenge was over, they couldn't visit the project site for another eight days. The New Zealand Police autopsy and investigation report had also been submitted directly to them. Dirk Jackson and a junior partner of the firm were flying in to see the project and meet with the staff and children in two days. Father Brennan and Sarah told Stephen that they could be contacted as local references.

Olivia decided to take a different approach with Hannah. "Meet me at the western corner near the gymnasium in fifteen minutes. No questions. Just be there," she said and hung up.

The western corner had been cleared for athletics and nature walks. The sun was shining brightly, and everything was washed clean from the rain the day before. Hannah slowed her walk, breathing in the fresh air, listening to the birds, and watching as the students played with a soccer ball in the field. Olivia waved a red flag to catch her attention. As she approached the trees, she saw Olivia had brought their bows and arrows, and attached targets at fifty- and seventy-five-foot intervals.

Hannah sighed, "It seems like forever since we had time for archery."

"No time like the present," Olivia responded. "Both of us could use some exercise and space away from the all-consuming project of ours."

Hannah's mind kept circling around Gustav and how he had almost crushed her dream with malicious vengeance and arrogance. She pulled out three arrows and quickly shot them directly into the center of the seventy-five-foot target.

"Wow! Now I know what the phrase 'Dead in the black' means. Seeing Gustav's face out there?" Olivia asked.

"Yeah. You don't really know what people are capable of until they act. I'm so thankful we both have a strong set of core values. Let's give our arms a workout."

They talked of homey things as they selected their targets and began their rounds. They collected arrows seven times before Hannah called a halt. "I won't be able to move my arms tomorrow if we keep this up. But I didn't realize how much I missed doing this with you."

"I'm getting sore already," Olivia said. "But I really needed to be outside, and archery helps me to focus. No need for us to turn into desk jockeys."

"You are a very intelligent and wonderful person. Thanks for kidnapping me today," Hannah said as she gave Olivia a hug. "Join me for a glass of wine?"

"Ah, you temptress! I need to help Stephen prepare for the lawyers. Raincheck?"

"Any time," Hannah said. They took down the targets, packed their arrows, and unstrung their bows before putting them in their lockers in the staff building.

$\star\ \star\ \star$

Logan was sent to Queenstown to pick up the lawyers from the airport. He waited for them to clear security checks and met them at the exit doors. They greeted him with smiles but remained reserved. As they drove away, Logan pointed out some of the local highlights, including the Technology Institute, the Music Center, and the beautiful churches. The lawyers listened attentively, asking questions and noticing the renovated business district. Logan called Hannah to report they were on their way and should be there in about an hour.

The junior partner, Edward Simmons, was a man in his late twenties, with blond hair, a bushy mustache, and broad shoulders. He asked Logan what it was like for him as part of the project.

Logan was hesitant to respond but wanted to convey how much good the project was accomplishing as well as the disappointments they faced. "The children and their families, the teachers, the administrators and medical staff— all these people are committed to changing our world view. Watching the children expand their abilities and helping each other is an inspiration for me. Even when they fail at the tasks they set for themselves, they gain knowledge and are excited to move on. My peers are the ones who have shown me how much I need to change."

"Really, I didn't want a sales pitch! I want to know about your role in the project and how it is affecting you. The recent incident is cause for grave concern," Edward insisted.

"I *am* being honest with you. This project is something brand-new. I fulfill different roles as the situations change. Sometimes I am a counselor; sometimes I'm a handyman; sometimes I'm a shoulder to cry on. We have learned to ask questions. The questions seem to open a new insight or pathway. It is what good teachers do for their students, but I don't lead them, they lead themselves. And ..."

Dirk Jackson's deep voice interrupted Logan. "You haven't talked about the tragic incident that occurred, and that's the main reason for our visit. Logan, how could something like that happen?"

Logan thought about what he could say to help them understand. "Are you married, Mr. Jackson?" he asked.

"What's that got to do with anything?" Dirk snapped.

"Please, work with me for a little while. How long did it take for you to know your girlfriend before you asked her to marry you?"

"A little more than two years," Dirk replied.

"And after you married her, did it surprise you when you discovered things about her that you didn't know?" Logan asked.

"I was surprised many times. And I discovered things about myself, from her perspective, that were just as surprising," Dirk replied.

"It was like that for us in the project. We didn't have a lot of time to get to know each other before we needed to get it going. There are aspects to all of us that we are just now experiencing. One thing I know about human beings is that we make mistakes. We often try our very best, but mistakes will still happen." Logan did not want to say more and perhaps jeopardize the project further. "That is my perspective, for what it's worth. You will need to ask the Management Team the rest of your questions. We're almost there."

Olivia and Stephen met the lawyers when they arrived. After introductions, they brought them to vacant rooms in the staff dormitory to unpack and get settled in. Olivia showed them a map of the facilities and invited them to walk the grounds. Lunch was available in the commissary. Their first meeting would be at 2 p.m. in the Lake Conference Room. Stephen asked if they needed anything else. They both shook their heads.

"Thank you," Edward said. "We look forward to meeting with you and your team this afternoon. This is an incredible facility, and I am eager to go exploring."

"If you have any questions, don't hesitate to call us. We can assign one of the staff to guide you, if you prefer," Olivia said.

"We'll be fine. We just need a little time to adjust. And please tell Logan that we appreciate his assistance," Dirk said.

Two o'clock arrived quickly and the Management Team was seated in the conference room when the lawyers arrived. Olivia began the introductions, and Nick set up the presentation. Lei Chen narrated the video information from the project drone and Gustav's drone as well. M'gera and Logan came in to discuss the evidence they found in the forest that was confirmed by the New Zealand Police official report. Olivia went over the results of the chemical tests. The lawyers did not interrupt but sat quietly taking notes. Hannah could see how upset they were becoming as the presentation continued.

Finally, Dirk looked at Hannah and said, "It's good to see you again, Hannah. You've been conspicuously silent. This project is your responsibility. What do you have to say?"

Hannah stood, walking over to the lights and motioning for Nick to turn off the computer. She looked over at Maya, who winked at her and smiled encouragement.

"How much do you know about Robert Langer, gentlemen?" she asked.

The lawyers looked at each other, puzzled by her question. Edward said, "He was immensely successful in business and has traveled widely. Robert is still making money with his products around the world. We were only selected to monitor this specific endowment."

"In other words, you do not know him," Hannah concluded. "I knew him when he was a shy, young man, just starting out on his life's journey. He lacked support, encouragement, and confidence. Somehow, I was able to convince him that nothing was beyond his reach." She paused in her narrative and walked to the window overlooking the lake.

"Do you know how many times he failed? It took him almost fifteen years to perfect his first idea and to see it manufactured, tested, and used to decrease human suffering. What would have happened if his financial backers lost confidence in him, just when he was on the verge of success?" She looked at her team, who were smiling at her, and then turned to the lawyers.

"It could be many years before the results of this project can make the changes needed for the world to survive. There will be many failures, disappointments, and challenges to overcome. But if we are not allowed to continue, using the funds Robert gave to us, the world will continue to be ruled by power wielded by wealthy, selfish people. This is an innovative project that aligns with Robert's hopeful vision for the world. And more than that, this project, the people here, and what we can achieve together are desperately needed if humanity is going to survive. The gifts these children and staff possess must be nurtured and encouraged, not squashed by rigidity, fear, and ignorance." Hannah was breathless with her vision and her passion.

Every person in the conference room was silent, Hannah's words ringing in their ears. Nick stood and went to Hannah's side. "Gentlemen, I suggest that we break for today. There is a lot of information to consider. Father Brennan, Sister Angelique, and Sarah Marie Dowie are members of the local community who are available if you want to talk to them. We will meet again tomorrow morning at 10 a.m. Enjoy your evening, and thank you for coming to see us."

The lawyers stood up to shake hands with the team, and then everyone slowly filed out of the conference room. Maya linked elbows with Edward, offering to show him around. Nick pulled Hannah aside and hugged her.

"You were wonderful!" he told her. "I wouldn't be surprised if they decide to invest in this project themselves."

"I don't know how the words came to me. I researched Robert's work over the past two days. He is an amazing man. He challenged me to help make the world a better, more compassionate place. And I think we found the way."

"We should name this project after him: 'Robert Langer's Search for XL-ENCE.' What do you think?" Nick asked.

"I think he will be proud of us." Hannah nodded. "I need to take a walk and calm my thoughts. See you later at dinner?"

"I'll cook at your place. Dinner at 7," Nick said.

Hannah walked to the edge of the facilities near the start of the forest. She allowed herself to be in the moment, sitting on a fallen tree trunk, staring into the shadows as the sun set behind her. She savored the crisp scent of the pine trees, the colors of the setting sun, and the sound of the birds, happily chattering to each other. She released all worries and fears about the future. She let herself be ... just Hannah.

The next morning, when Dirk Jackson met with the Management Team, he had only one thing to say. "Don't stop. I believe you did the best you could in a very dangerous situation. We'll talk with Stephen about managing the remainder of the funds. But I think Robert is proud of you, Hannah," Dirk smiled and enthusiastically shook her hand.

The Management Team applauded, smiling with relief and glad to show appreciation for their leader.

Olivia offered to drive the lawyers back to Queenstown after lunch. They agreed and went back to their rooms to pack. The rest of the Management Team excused themselves to get back to work with the staff and children. Hannah walked over to Maya, who kissed her on both cheeks and wrapped her in a big hug.

Hannah was reluctant to let go, but she had work to do as well. "You know what? I miss Grams and Grandpa Neil. Do you think I could convince them to come for a visit?"

"Hannah, you could convince monkeys to fly if you put your mind to it. Why not? They would want to meet your special guy," she suggested slyly.

"You always know everything, don't you?" Hannah said.

"It's what families do." Maya stroked her cheek and then walked over to the Music building to check in on Chelsea.

Epilogue

Dear Hannah,

Congratulations! You're off to a good start. But there is always the other side. It's time to take on the bad guys. The biggest polluters, defilers, and greedy conglomerates won't be so easily defeated. To help you in the newest challenge, I have prepared a gift for you.

His name is Spot, after my childhood pet Australian shepherd. He is an AI robot, with extraordinary data storage capacity. You will need his help as the tipping point gets closer. Only by shutting down some of these corporate pulverizers can you slow the irreversible damage to the Earth.

Of course, you will need more money to do this. Remember, money is the great equalizer in the game of corporate politics. $100 billion should give you enough clout. Once again, the lawyers will be the judge of your counteroffensive strategy. Use your resources wisely. The children are growing quickly—and so are their skills.

I suggest that you start researching this challenge and send the Accelerators and children to look for Spot. I have faith in you all.
Your friend,
Robert Langer

Acknowledgments

First, I must acknowledge the Women in Publishing Summit of 2024. The speakers, presenters, software designers, editors, and writers who told me about their journeys helped me to take the steps to make publication of XL-ENCE possible.

My beta readers, Mary Frances Hill, Mary Ann Heimann, and John Steiner, provided me with great insight, constructive criticism, and support.

Although this book is a work of fiction, it presents a possible road to heal our planet, the animals, plants, and people, in both new and old ways. This is me, reaching out to you, in hopes that we can take these next steps together.

About the Author

Patti Mobile grew up with stories--bedtime stories, family history, story books, and comic books. Her favorite family story was about how her father's mother, Nana, traveled from Russia, across the Pacific Ocean, landing in San Francisco. She was only fourteen years old, and she was put on many trains by strangers who looked out for her and helped her to find her future husband and his siblings in New York. Storytelling is an art.

It captures our imagination, and it helps us to understand each other and our world.

Patti's story has both successes and failures. She was a competitive athlete from her twenties to her sixties. She received the Most Valuable Player Award at the National Volleyball Championships in Minneapolis, Minnesota, in 2003 when she was fifty years old. Today Patti lives in Long Beach, California, with her husband, Alex, where they enjoy growing vegetables, herbs, and fruit. They also have two telescopes that show them the ever-changing universe filled with wonders.

Patti wanted to share her stories with other people, perhaps to inspire them to write and share their own stories. She says that one of the things that makes us unique is our creativity. We express that creativity through art, photography, cooking, clothing design, music, tools, and telling stories. She hopes that your journey through her imagination will be enlightening and entertaining. Safe travels!